No Treasure 1

GW01159341

Paul To

NO TREASURE FOR THE BRAVE

First edition. October 21, 2024.

ISBN: 979-8227601896

Written by Paul Toskiam.

Also by Paul Toskiam

Warning

This book is a work of fiction. Names, characters, places, and incidents are products of the author's imagination and are used fictitiously. Any resemblance to actual persons, living or dead, events, or locales is entirely coincidental.

This book is not to be used as a source of information or advice. The author and publisher of this novel accept no responsibility for any damage caused by reading this novel.

This novel is intended for adults over the legal age of majority in the country of purchase, and contains scenes that may be shocking to some readers.

That morning

I had a strange dream last night. No. A terrifying dream. A real nightmare. I was lying on my back, in the middle of the street, a street without asphalt, with dust on the ground. I was on my back, feeling the taste of blood in my mouth and staring up at the sky: a pristine blue sky. There I was, unable to move. I was trapped in my body. All I heard was the engine of a big truck revving up close to me and speeding away, raising a cloud of dust that fell on me, in my eyes. I screamed, but I still couldn't move.

I think that's what woke me up.

Fantastic, I must have spent the night snoring like a hibernating bear. I feel like I've got a whole field of absorbent cotton in my mouth. My face is numb, like after a night spent on a pimpled pillow. Then reality hits me like a comet: I'm still alive. The whole universe has agreed that my time on Earth should last a little longer. All right, universe, I'll see what I can do not to disappoint you.

With all the grace of a short-sighted panda, I try to open one eye, but a little hitch has been added to the list of my morning woes. My eyelid had fun sticking to my eye while I was sleeping. My eyelid leads a very creative life. The dry air may have contributed to this nocturnal collage.

With a flick of my tongue, as controlled as a cat smoothing its fur, I generate a thin trickle of saliva on my index finger. With a lacemaker's delicacy, I bring my index finger closer and moisten my recalcitrant eyelid. I take these maniacal precautions because, alas, I've already experienced the pain of a stuck eyelid that suddenly opens up and rips off half the surface of the eye. And as we tend to blink a lot in such

2

moments, the pain becomes almost exquisite, so unbearable is it. It's a solo performance, with an empty room, that I'd rather not play again.

I finally open my eyes properly, with no major disaster.

For a few moments, the room I'm in seems foreign to me. It's a good-sized room, decorated with simplicity yet practicality: a large double bed in the center, its thick mattress offering sufficient but unadorned comfort, a solitary desk, two armchairs on either side of a modest coffee table, then a wardrobe leaning against the opposite wall. A narrow corridor leads to a half-open door, revealing a bathroom. The room is lit by a soft, warm light. I'm in a hotel room, just as I was looking for the familiar landmarks of my studio.

Cautiously, I leave the warmth of the bed and place my feet on the slippery floor. My feet are slipping on water. No sooner have I moved than a rustle reaches my ears. There's movement in the bed, grunting. My neck rebels and locks as I reluctantly turn my head to see what's going on behind me. A woman, whose face I don't recognize, lies in my bed. Her

long platinum-blond hair is splayed across the pillow. A rebellious curl falls over her angelic face. She opens her eyes - no eyelid problems, her - and smiles at me with a happy, satisfied expression. How could I have failed to notice this beauty of nature when I examined the room? It's fascinating what the mind can choose to perceive, leaving everything else aside.

The young woman lets out a contented sigh, like a purring cat, before turning over and drifting peacefully back to sleep. The question on my lips refuses to be silenced: who is she? My mind tries hard to remember, but to no avail. I'm not a morning person, and all I can think about is what I see. She seems perfectly at ease in this room, as if she's always owned it. She seems to have had a good time. Thanks to me, perhaps? It certainly must be, since she's in my bed. Well, let's not exaggerate: in the same bed as me.

I get up, slowly, avoiding slipping, doing my best not to interrupt the peaceful slumber of the sleeping beauty beside me. With a silent thief's gait, I slip into the bathroom, still tired but curiously euphoric. I turn on the tap and fresh water gurgles happily into the sink, a morning symphony welcoming the start of a promising new day.

The face in the mirror stares back at me. It's a mixture of exhaustion, confusion and excitement painted on a dark backdrop with contours hollowed out by a restless night. I push back the rebellious lock of hair that dances across my forehead like a spring and prepare to investigate the bizarre contortions my neck claims to have undergone during the night. Always listen to your neck. It's a faithful indicator.

The sharp pain, which pierces my neck and all the way to my jaw, does indeed resemble the remains of a clumsy adventurer tumbling down the stairs, head first. I laugh, immediately regretting my audacity as the pain doubles with each jerk of my laughter.

I gradually recall fragments of the previous evening. I spent some time at the hotel bar, alone, with no real cause for celebration. The aim was to escape the hassles of everyday life, the fact that I no longer had a job and didn't know what I was going to do with the rest of my life. However, I don't remember running into this young woman who seems to be in full bloom here. Did we exchange a few words? What did we talk about? Did we get close? I mean, how many times did we fuck? That's all I know. But my deep sleep is a valid clue.

I return silently to the bedroom and sit on the edge of the bed, watching the young woman who is still sleeping peacefully. She doesn't react to the little noise I make. She doesn't even grunt when my fat ass pressed against the edge makes her slide a little towards me. That's a second clue. Her face is relaxed and radiant, almost innocent. I wonder who she really is? What are her passions? What are her dreams and what makes her happy in general? But all these questions remain unanswered for the moment.

My gaze falls mechanically on my cell phone on the bedside table. Perhaps I'll find some clues about this enigmatic blonde? I rummage through my messages and contacts, looking for her name or anything else that might help me track her down. But nothing. Not even an unknown number. No photos, no videos to remind me of what happened and how I got to this room. Unless I didn't have time to capture anything?

Ah, a voicemail. Who leaves voicemails anymore?

"Hello Mr. Oscar Spicas. I'm Steven McLuman from Premium Genius. I've reviewed your profile and have a unique opportunity for you. If you're listening to the market, please don't hesitate to contact me..."

My profile? It's from before the creation of the world... Another one of those panicked headhunters... If it pays well...

Ah, another text message this time: *"Oscar, the bank called again. Apparently you haven't cleared your overdraft this month. If you need money, call me."*

It's mom. She makes up stuff to get me to call her, again...

For the time being, and instead of torturing my mind with unanswered questions, I've decided to take things as they come. I'll get to the bottom of it later. Maybe during the day, additional memories will surface in my mind and give me a glimpse of this night? If not, I don't care. That's always been my policy: as long as I'm alive, life's good!

In the meantime, I'm simply going to take advantage of this moment of calm to go downstairs for breakfast. With my little veteran's savings, it's a luxury I can still afford. I put on my clothes, which smell strongly of cold sweat and alcohol: soft, loose-fitting sand-colored pants, a flashy, soft, loose-fitting white shirt, and sports shoes that I often wear as sandals, crushing the back, the heel, well, ... Got it? I hate clothes that compress the body. If you ever want to buy me something, choose anything that's loose-fitting! No, I'm not fat. I'm heavy. It's not the same at all.

This is it. Out the door. I make a special effort to close the door without slamming it. I'm a gentleman. I stand in the corridor and walk the few steps to the elevator door.

My footsteps make no sound on this dark red carpet with gold edging on the sides. I stand there, waiting calmly in front of the elevator doors. My hands tremble slightly. You know, that little tremor that sometimes starts without you really knowing why. Sometimes it's after carrying a heavy load. I carried something heavy? Crap. And that little patch of dried blood on your abdomen, like smeared lipstick? That's painful, too. I'm a morning pain all by myself.

My mind is in a complete fog. Strangely enough, my hands have a life of their own this morning. It's as if they're acting as a sensor in the face of imminent danger. My eyes feverishly scan the illuminated buttons on the elevator control panel. I don't know why I stare at this panel for thirty seconds. Ah, yes, I am: I'm not a morning person.

I finally press the first floor button with the back of my index finger. I don't really like touching surfaces that everyone else is touching. And most of all, there are weird people licking anything while filming themselves now. The world is going badly, very badly.

Finally, the elevator starts moving and arrives at my floor. I thought those buttons weren't connected to any electrical circuit. It happens all the time. Especially since this neighborhood has taken several raids in a row. They've patched things up, but sometimes they pop. The doors slide silently open, revealing an old woman inside.

Shit, an old lady. No, it's not that. Growing old is a blessing. Especially today with all these... She's very well dressed, this old lady. It's obvious. Her impeccable, sophisticated look immediately attracts my attention and prompts me to contemplate her in detail. Her skin is thin and stretched, just between her forehead and chin. I smile. She thinks it's a greeting. The cunt. If she only knew. She's wearing an elegant deep-black dress, something that absorbs all the subdued light in the elevator cab. Her delicate embroidered collar and super complicated chignon give her a very intriguing medieval air. She must have beautiful long hair once that bun is undone. My eyes then land on the luxurious handbag she holds firmly at her side. The bag tells the whole story of its wearer. Reinforced with patinated metal and set with small stones around the edges, it tells the story of rivers of dough. An avalanche of money! These old ladies are terrible. Real thieving magpies. Well, I don't know about that. She looks like she's spent the night with a gigolo. In any case, she reeks of perfume, very pampering, too, of which she must have poured half a bottle over herself. No doubt to mask the old lady smell that has begun to gnaw at her? Or maybe she's just like me. In the morning, she doesn't wash. So she perfumes herself. That's how elevators are hell on the nose.

"Are you getting off?" she asks, as if waiting for my answer to press a floor button.

What a silly question. Yes, I'll be right down, ma'am. Borrowing an elevator is often surrounded by a panoply of banalities that tire me and that I'll spare you here. I'm a good soul. Yet she can't resist mentioning the bad weather earlier this morning, with the heavy rain that woke her up by tapping on her window. Out of humanism, I'm the one who's very concerned about this problem of driving rain on the windows. I meet her gaze in the mirror several times, as if she's following me, as if she's measuring the quality of my attention to her nonsense. Old people need regular signs that they're still with us.

Despite my best efforts, she doesn't seem convinced. Suddenly, I see her skinny, veiny hand emerge from her expensive bag with a revolver dangling from the end. It's one of those models you only see in old cowboy movies anymore. His now icy gaze fixes on me, inviting me to keep quiet and follow his instructions without question. For a second, I panic. A gun in such an old hand: the shot could go off on its own at any moment.

"Shut up!"

I look at her with real interest this time. But this time, she doesn't care. I haven't said a word for at least two minutes and she's asking me to be quiet? I'm more and more afraid that her gun will fire on its own. The floor indicator shows the fifth floor. We're almost at the first floor.

"Don't make any sudden movements. Stay calm and cooperate. We have business to settle."

Suddenly she comes up to me, grabs my jaw as if to force it open and I understand, half hilariously, that she's trying to shove the barrel of her revolver into my mouth.

I'm two heads taller than her and probably forty years younger. I'll let you imagine the pathetic scene. She stands trembling against me on tiptoe. And she's looking for the entrance to my mouth, which I don't open because my jaw is sore and I want to spare her. Her barrel scrapes all my front teeth and finally slides against my nose, curling it upwards. Our gazes synchronize, long and unblinking. I step back, slowly, showing her my hands to reassure her. I ask her almost in a whisper:

"Who are you? What do you want from me?"

"The questions will come later. For now, follow me," she commands with a wave of her revolver.

She has a fine ear for an old woman. The elevator doors open with no one in front of us. We quickly cross the hotel lobby, attracting a few curious glances. The old lady and I make our way to the exit door, where a chauffeur in an impeccable suit and cap awaits us. The old lady intrigues me more and more as we approach the luxurious black limousine parked just ahead.

"Madame, everything is ready," says the chauffeur, executing a regulation bow.

"Perfect. We're to drive Monsieur Oscar to his destination. Make sure there are no problems on our way."

"Of course, Madame."

Does the old lady know my first name? I'm shoved roughly inside the limousine, the doors closing with a dull slam. This driver sure knows how to treat a guest like a sack of potatoes.

As the car starts, I realize that my life has just taken an unexpected turn, both frightening and mysterious. And I have to admit, I hadn't planned this kind of breakfast.

The old woman remains silent, her gaze staring straight ahead. I try to gather my thoughts, to understand what's going on. Can I escape?

She has an enigmatic smile on her lips. She's sitting on my right in the back of the car. She's still pointing her gun at me with her hooked hand.

"My dear Oscar, you are much more special than you realize. The answers you seek are at our destination. Just wait a little longer. They will be revealed to you."

Silence reigns in the car, disturbed only by the steady purr of the engine. I'm terrified and at the same time fascinated by this old woman with her calm mask and delicious sophistication. Who is she really? Why has she chosen me? This is the second woman I've failed to identify all day. When will the third come along?

My heart pumps in my chest like it's trying to pump oil. I'm looking for an opportunity to escape. I know I have to act quickly while we're stopped at a red light. Taking a deep breath, I grab the door handle and open it, ready to flee.

"Oh, how original. No. Be patient, Oscar. You won't regret what awaits you," she says in her sarcasm-tinged voice.

I freeze in place. I turn slowly to see the old woman smiling at me. She's still holding the gun.

"You really think you can outrun me, Oscar?" she scoffs.

She giggles darkly. A laugh that sends her bouncing across the back seat and I feel under my buttocks. And it goes on for several seconds, as if she knows some secret about my fate that I don't yet know. I hate people who know what's going to happen to you before you do. They're birds of ill omen. She continues, with little hand gestures:

"Oh, Oscar. Trust me, running away won't get you anywhere."

I pretend to calm down. I mean, so as not to tear her down on the spot. Maybe what she has to tell me is interesting after all? She smiles at me again, this time benevolently. She's a good actress. She looks like she's been doing it for centuries. What's more - I can see it in her mischievous eyes - she immediately understands that I'm not going to give in and that I'm going to try again. I can easily read it in her squinted eyes, like two horizontal lines. And she reads mine, to make sure she puts a bullet between my eyes if I get too creative.

I scan the horizon and surroundings with false confidence, diverting my opponent's attention. Then I lunge forward like a leaping cheetah, hoping to take her by surprise. Miraculously, I manage to make her drop her weapon. But before I can even savor my victory, the old lady reacts in a split second. She throws me a kick in the chest worthy of a champion boxing kangaroo. Holy shit! I stumble backwards, my head hitting the door window. It makes a noise that echoes in my gut and wakes up the pain in my jaw. This crazy woman is a walking disaster. But when she hits, it hurts, it really hurts. But where does she get all that energy? She's got a real talent for it. It's like she's been doing it for centuries.

She stands over me and her eyes burn with rage like a flaming hut. Her face has become frightening. No, I'm sorry: it's downright terrifying. That grimace that came out of nowhere makes her look like an evil dragon about to unleash an infernal flame. While I'm transfixed by this raging head, I forget that this viper has taken up his gun. She threatens to turn my skull into a jigsaw puzzle with the butt she uses like a hammer to calm me down.

I look into her eyes again as if to say "fuck you, you old crone" and I understand that she wants to calm me down, but not to finish me off. Interesting. So I have real value in her eyes? Frankly, just out of curiosity, I'd like to fast-forward to see where this old hag wants to take me with such insistence. Alas, I'll have to knock him out permanently if I'm to get out of here in one piece.

I'm pondering the ultimate escape, when a deafening screech pierces the air behind us. It's a motorcycle, appearing out of nowhere, slaloming in our direction at dizzying speed between the inert cars. The driver, dressed all in black, rushes towards us, pressed up against her bike. She soon stops next to me, in complete control of her heavy machine. She approaches the door, puts something on it and drives off a few yards. From inside, we watch as the door explodes, releasing thick grey smoke and the smell of electrocution. The woman comes back to the car, revving her bike's engine. Without any difficulty, she opens the door on my side and hands me a helmet.

"Quick, get in!" she cries with desperation in her voice, as if her life depended on it.

Frankly, I'm not the type to accept an invitation from a stranger. But I don't know what's going on: I put on my helmet and prepare to leap onto the back of this providential motorcycle.

Of course, the old hag tries to hold me back. Her razor-sharp black fingernails dig into my clothes, ravaging my skin, while deep scratches mark my abdomen and hips, spreading insidious pain. This dragon's strength is unprecedented.

An evil glow lights up the driver's gaze as he weaves between the seats, animated by a bloodthirsty frenzy. His fists rain blows on my head, an avalanche of brutal assaults that shake my skull with every impact. With inhuman strength, he viciously pulls me by the feet, trying to tear me away from any hope of escape.

Exhaustion slowly consumes me, but my survival instinct kicks in. Without further hesitation, I unleash my fury. In a final wild escape, I deliver a devastating kick, striking the old hag's deformed face. Her cheekbone bursts under the violence of my blow, and she is propelled like a disjointed puppet against the rear window, leaving a bloodstain in her wake.

The driver plunges back towards me to finish me off. His complexion is already red and darkens further, revealing his insatiable rage. Without mercy, I smash his head with a masterly blow from my helmet, resonating like a major percussive blow in this fateful symphony, in the confined space of this cursed car. A strange satisfaction washes over me as my assailant's skull sinks, staining the passenger compartment with his scattered brains. It's a fighter's satisfaction. A hard drug I wouldn't recommend to anyone.

My final kick, of unspeakable brutality, completes the gruesome dance of death. The driver, reduced to a broken puppet, collapses in a pool of blood and despair, while my own impulse catapults me out of this terrifying vehicle, finally freeing my soul from the clutches of this waking nightmare.

I close the door, to be polite, and jump on the back of the bike as if I'd been doing it all my life. I hold on tight as the bike's wheels screech on the asphalt and we're soon speeding away, leaving my two captors' car in the dust and a chorus of horns.

Yes, you're right: I know how to fight. After that workout, I think I'm finally fully awake. I'm not a morning person. And I'm not one for early-morning nagging!

As we speed through the city streets, I crash into the third unknown woman of my morning who is riding this motorcycle at an unreasonable speed. I press myself up against her to avoid being ejected in mid-race. I hear her panting breath through the helmet and feel her lungs filling and emptying at a breathless pace. Frankly, I'm impressed:

"For a tornado that came out of nowhere, you're incredibly talented," I said in a blasé tone, as if she were taking her motorcycle license and I were her instructor.

She laughs, with a deep, contagious sound.

"Well, I couldn't let you get torn apart by that crazy old woman, could I?"

I let out a nervous laugh. Everyone seems to know me this morning. Is it just me who doesn't understand what's going on?

"So, can I know your name?", I ask her, curious about the one who just saved me.

She lets a few seconds pass while we take a corner at full speed, bent over, almost touching the ground with our knees.

"Call me, Lola. And believe me, Oscar, this is just the beginning of the adventure."

Adventure? I don't need adventure. I need peace and quiet. I hope I don't need to break her skull too!

I get a little lost in my thoughts and let myself be carried along - not much of a choice - through the streets that unfold in this morning atmosphere. I notice that Lola has made a long U-turn through the city to finally bring me back to the hotel. She parks in a side street and we get off her big motorcycle, which she probably hasn't washed in months.

"How do you know my first name?"

"Oh, that's easy: you spent the night with my sister!"

I must be making a blatant face of surprise, even with my cheeks compressed in this helmet, because she continues:

"It's all right. I'm not here to scold you. No, actually I need your help. Clara's in danger."

She speeds up again, as if inviting me to keep my mouth shut without telling me. Soon we're near the hotel. Lola stops her bike in the next street.

So I spent the night with Clara. Lola's sister's name is Clara. I take off my helmet and make a face to show my surprise, and Lola bursts out laughing.

In turn, she removes her helmet and shakes her long blond hair, like her sister's. Her hair never ceases to unfurl out of the helmet, as if carried by a gust of wind. Her hair keeps blowing out of the helmet, as if carried by a gust of wind. But there's no wind.

Before my contemplative eyes, she arranges the two helmets with calculated precision as if he were depositing jewels in a safe. She keeps a wary eye on passers-by in the street. What's she afraid of? That passers-by will turn into hungry monsters at any moment? At the same time, I did get kidnapped by an old lady who apparently only wanted the best for me... I couldn't get over the old lady with the gun.

In the middle of a conference with myself, I didn't notice Lola watching me silently from the other side of the bike. She smiles and skirts around the bike to get closer to me until she brushes against me, then touches me. She smiles again, as if she wants me to smile too. Almost as if she wanted to order me to open my mouth and enjoy my perfect teeth. She must think I'm a horse she's about to buy at full price? She moves even closer, as if that were possible, until she touches my nose with the tip of hers. I feel her breath on my lips. I'm lucky: her breath is bearable. Not super fresh either, but hey, I'll survive. I recoil instinctively - of course - who wouldn't do that when faced with a stranger trying to caress your nose with hers?

"Open your mouth!" she orders with conviction.

Oh, okay. I like opening my mouth in front of strangers. It's always fun to follow other people's strange preferences, isn't it? Then again, maybe this is the start of a new fashion trend: "Opening your mouth in public".

But I digress. She then reassures me that she has no intention of raping me. Ah well, so much the better, I'm indeed reassured! Why would she need to see the inside of my mouth, anyway? Is she trying to confirm that I have indeed swallowed a whole row of bottles in more or less mismatched colors?

Anyway, I obey her curious request. Probably because she's a very pretty woman? Because, let's be honest, I'm a bit hypnotized by her irresistible charisma. Her hair, her slender, feline body, her character as an asshole who grows balls and thinks she can do anything... I'm under her spell. I even invented that non-existent wind in her hair. I'm the first to be astonished, but I'm well and truly in her thrall. Or maybe I've been feeling indebted to her ever since she saved me from my kidnapping... which never happened? Or maybe it's because I unwittingly crossed swords with her sister during a lively evening that I've forgotten all about? Or even that we fucked all night, as Lola claims? No, I'm not particularly obsessed with it. But at the moment, there's a shortage of males and women are less fussy. And that's a fact. You'll soon understand what I'm talking about.

Anyway, while I'm lost in these sterile considerations, I realize that she's examining my mouth as if she were at home: like a dentist looking for billing. She's fumbling in every nook and cranny, lifting my cheek with surgical

dexterity and attention. Has she been doing this all her life?

And that's it, she's done. She stares at me out of the corner of her eye. "I thought so," she declares before leaving without looking back, like a superheroine on her next mission to defend the planet. In her movement, she beckons me to follow her with a curt hand gesture, because clearly: I've mastered sign language perfectly.

While I follow her like a gentle poodle, I remain perplexed. What could this woman - well aware of her natural charms - possibly be looking for in my mouth? And above all, what could I have done last night to find myself embroiled with all those enraged people?

PAUL TOSKIAM

The bracelet

Victor and Adrien were in Adrien's room. Adrien's parents had gone away for the weekend and the two boys were home alone.

Adrien was angry. In fact, completely furious. He asked Victor to return the bracelet Sandra had just given him. A vulgar bracelet made of two black leather straps with no market value. But with an emotional value that had just driven Adrien completely mad. Victor replied nervously: "Why do you care so much about this fucking bracelet? You're a pain in the ass. It's mine now. Sandra gave it to me."

Adrien looked Victor straight in the eye and said in a firm, threatening tone, "That's not true, she gave it to me and I want it back, now!" he asserted as a matter of course, with a brisk wave of his arm, as if he'd just cracked a whip, index finger pointed at the ground.

Victor, ready to take up the challenge, replied nonchalantly: "You can just try and take it away from me!"

Without further ado, Adrien threw himself brutally at Victor. The two teenagers engaged in a sudden, violent and merciless brawl. Blows rained down and the sound of overturned furniture mingled with their cries of rage and pain.

In the midst of this confrontation, dictated by honor and virility, Adrien managed to immobilize Victor's arm and angrily retorted: "You're going to give me back that bracelet now, or I swear you're going to regret it!"

Victor, out of breath, refused to return the bracelet.

Adrien looked at Victor, his eyes filled with anger and jealousy. He couldn't understand why Sandra had given Victor this "magnificent" bracelet. They were supposed to be friends, weren't they? "Why him and not me?" he wondered.

Adrien was seething inside. He felt betrayed, betrayed by Sandra, betrayed by Victor. He couldn't bear the idea that Victor might have something he didn't have. Especially something from Sandra. He approached Victor, fists clenched.

"Give me back that bracelet, Victor. It doesn't belong to you," he threatened again in a tight voice.

Victor stepped back, startled by Adrien's sudden aggression and the fact that he was no longer holding back his blows. He'd never seen him like this. "Sandra gave it to me. It's mine now. You don't get to tell me what to do!"

The tension rose a notch. Adrien felt anger invade him. This anger that becomes your master and controls you. It was something much stronger than him. And he had to unleash all that fury. He wasn't going to let Victor get away with it. Adrien reached out to grab the bracelet, but Victor deftly dodged. They stared into each other's eyes again, like two wild beasts challenging each other before the final assault. Consequences no longer mattered. There was only one to go.

The two young men rushed at each other, crossing the room in a tumult of rumbles and shocks. Furniture wobbled one after the other, objects flew. They were both prisoners of their unhealthy will to win, to show their superiority.

The confrontation lasted several long minutes, until finally, exhausted and out of breath, they parted. Silence fell over the house, broken only by the sound of their panting breaths, like two exhausted dogs.

Hoping to find refuge, Victor ran up the steps of the grand staircase to the third floor. His heart threatened to give way. He knew he was trapped in front of Adrien, who had turned into a ferocious beast with a wounded sense of self-esteem. But he had no choice. He had to find a solution. Victor could already hear the sound of footsteps behind him, trying to catch up. He knew his adversary would not give up.

Victor dragged himself breathless to the back of the large living room, where the large open third-floor window stood. He turned and, as expected, saw Adrien's head, then his whole body, emerge from the perspective of the staircase, sweating like a zombie emerging from the water, to approach inexorably.

"You'll go no further Victor," Adrien predicted in a menacing voice. "You're finished."

"I'm not finished as long as I'm breathing," Victor replied, trying to hide his fear.

Adrien had always been stronger than him, but Victor knew he couldn't give up. He had to defend himself, whatever the cost, for honor.

Adrien lunged at Victor, his gaze filled with hatred. Victor backed away until he was cornered against the window railing. He knew it was now or never. He had to fight for his life.

With an almost animal-like leap, Adrien charged at him and shoved him roughly through the window. Victor screamed as he fell, the wind whistling in his ears. He knew this fall would be fatal.

He braced himself for the impact, closed his eyes and felt the ground approaching at dizzying speed.

He smashed violently against a large, bare stone slab protruding from the lawn, feeling immense pain. He wanted to move his body to get up, but remained completely inert. He was like one of those half-awake dreams where you try to move, to scream, but no sound comes out of your throat. He tried to cry out for help, but no sound came from his mouth. He was alone, abandoned, and he knew this was the end. He was going to die for this bracelet.

Adrien watched his work from the third floor. Then he took the staircase again, striding down it, realizing with every step the atrocity of what he had just caused. He dreaded what he would find downstairs, but he had to face reality. He stormed up to the threshold of the house and found Victor's dislocated body lying on the floor. He shuddered with hope to see that his friend was still breathing.

"Victor," he murmured, kneeling beside him.

Victor painfully opened his eyes, the pain visible in his gaze, then coughed violently, coughing up a little blood.

Adrien felt a lump form in his stomach. Yet deep down, he was still furious. He was convinced that Victor had stolen Sandra, the love of his life. So, without thinking, giving in definitively to his destructive impulse, and without holding back his strength, he delivered a final kick to Victor's face, sending him sliding to the floor, blood spurting from his nose and broken teeth.

"Sandra will never want you again, hunchback!" spat Adrien contemptuously.

Victor, coughing and spitting blood, looked at him with eyes filled with fear and pain. "You're crazy, Adrien. Sandra hasn't loved you for a long time. It's over between you two," he stammered without really articulating and with an effort that caused him terrible pain. But it was enough for his friend Adrien to understand his words.

"You're lying!" roared Adrien. "She still loves me. It's because of you that she rejects me. And now you're going to pay for it!"

He was about to hit Victor again, but something stopped him.

Perhaps it was the look of terror in his former friend's eyes, or maybe a flash of lucidity in his own blinding anger. Whatever it was, Adrien held back. He wanted to finish off his rival. But he stopped, stood up and walked a few steps around his crippled, downed victim.

"No," he said at last. "I'll let you live," he added thoughtfully. "Your life will be hell. Sandra will never want you again. You'll be alone, rejected by everyone, condemned to live with your deformity for the rest of your life."

Victor stared at him, incredulous. "I don't love Sandra," he revealed in a breath that sounded like a rattle.

Adrien shook his head, trying to understand. "It doesn't matter. You've taken what's mine. But I'm letting you live. Now get out of my sight and never come back."

Victor didn't get up and lost consciousness.

Adrien left him there, inert, to his fate.

PAUL TOSKIAM

The hunchback

Room 618, Hotel Tonant

Lola turns the corner at a brisk pace, oblivious to the menacing presence of the tank as it creeps ominously forward, crushing the asphalt beneath its tracks. Suspicious, I hide against the front door of the building nearby. My heart skips a beat as the anxiety permeates every fibre of my being. This drawn-out war has left behind only a soiled landscape and bruised souls. And it has left me with a series of traumas I'll never be able to shake off. I can make out shreds of skin hanging grotesquely over the death vehicle. I try to suppress the horrors stirring in my thoughts, preferring to focus my mind on something else. I wait, holding my breath, for the rumble of the tank to subside. Eventually, it stops further away, then slides into an adjacent street, leaving behind a cloud of black smoke.

Without further ado, I rush towards the hotel entrance. It's less crowded than earlier, when the old lady with the revolver kindly invited me to follow her in her car, straight out of a collector's garage. No one is standing behind the deserted hotel counter. Lola, on the other hand, is waiting impatiently for me in front of the elevator. Her gaze pierces me and I read in it a hint of reproach at my tardiness.

"At last, here you are!" she exclaims, her words carrying barely a shadow of bitterness. "This elevator doesn't seem to be working..."

I offer him a smile laden with understanding. "The power's probably out. It happens a lot in the neighborhood, you know?"

She glares at me, clearly offended by my suggestion. I point out, "It's on the sixth floor, room 618."

"Well, come on then!" she invites me, before bolting for the stairs, without even waiting for me. These steps loom before us like merciless adversaries, but our will is unshakeable. Each step is taken with power, our legs muscling to the frantic rhythm of our ascent.

I know, I'm being a bit insistent, but that's just to show that I had no desire to climb those damn stairs on foot. As a consolation, I enjoyed every movement of Lola's blond hair sweeping across the top of her buttocks, like a hypnotic pendulum, filling me with electrifying tension, and stiff!

All right, then. You don't like my soldier humor?

Shit, she's got a head start and she's getting ready to charge down the sixth-floor corridor, her gaze fixed ahead, ready for anything. I don't know why she's charging down like that when her sister must still be fast asleep. Lola turns around, abruptly, heading straight for me and hitting me head-on on the stairs.

"Hey! Be careful!", I say, trying to regain my balance.

"Shhh... silence," she whispers to me in a low voice, bending down slightly and pointing at two individuals waiting outside room 618. Lola's face has become grave, marked by apprehension.

I ask her, "Shit. Who are those guys?", trying to understand the situation.

"Funny, I was going to ask you the same question," she replies, disappointed and pensive.

"Friends of Clara's, maybe?", I offer, hoping for an answer so we know what to expect.

"No, not really. She doesn't have any bald friends. Are you sure she was in the room when you went out this morning?" she questions in a whisper, raising a suspicion in me.

I take another few moments to think about it, trying to sort out my obsessions and the doubts sown by this fury.

"Yes, I'm sure of it. She was sleeping like a baby", I finally confirm, despite my growing uncertainties. Above all, I haven't had my coffee this morning. My head is still under the pillow.

"Then we've got a problem," she observes, pulling two knives out of who knows where at the speed of light. "You take the one on the left and I'll take the one on the right."

I freeze for a moment, unable to understand what she's asking me. What's going on here?

"You mean...", I'm unable to complete my question, finally realizing the deadly game she's offering me.

"Shhh... silence. They'll spot us. You know how to throw a knife, I hope?" she bellows, handing me one of the knives. The blade is all smooth and shiny. It's superbly balanced. I immediately understand that this woman also knows exactly what she's talking about when it comes to knife throwing.

I stammer as I climb into the treble: "No. Well, not too much. Maybe it's government guys?"

"Fuck, keep it down, dammit!" she mutters, visibly annoyed, and elbowing me copiously in the side. "Anyway, I need to get into this room. Clara needs me. Look what you've done...they're coming for us now.... You take the one on the left in five... four... three... two... now!"

We leap out into the corridor. Lola gets into position, like a javelin thrower. She stares intently at her target before throwing her knife with force, aiming directly at the head of the man on the right. The knife flies through the air, spinning in a precise trajectory, before finally crashing into the man's head. The man grunts, spins around several times holding his face, before collapsing like a lump with a thud onto the thick corridor carpet. It's clean. It's clean. It's the first time. Yes, she's been doing this all her life. I wonder who she really is and why she protects me like a mother? But I don't have time for further analysis.

"Oscar!" shouts Lola, urging me to act quickly on my own left target. Alas, it's already too late. The man is already on us and draws his weapon, a small automatic machine gun capable of slicing us up in a fraction of a second. I notice red on his shirt cuffs, like fresh blood. He's already worked this morning. A split second is all I need to pounce on him, rolling on his shins and shattering his legs with my full weight. He grunts, but his reaction is short-lived as his cut throat prevents him from expressing himself properly. I didn't give him a chance. I couldn't afford it. He just stands there, mouth wide open, throat wide open, eyes fixed on the ceiling. I hate doing this. I hate killing. I told you: it's a drug. But like you, I prefer to survive. I've barely had time to recover from my emotions when Lola takes the knife from me, wipes it diligently on the black suit of the guy with the throat cut and puts it away, I don't know where.

"Come, follow me, and quietly," Lola asks me cordially as she crouches towards the door of room 618. "I'm afraid for Clara," she adds.

Our eyes meet briefly in front of the bedroom door. I can see the fear in Lola's eyes. And in my own eyes, I assume she can read a growing awareness of the unexpected magnitude of this morning.

She addresses me with a series of signs that look like words I'm supposed to decipher and put back in order to understand. Annoyed, or rather despairing of the nullity of her partner in fortune - me - she whispers to me: "You enter the room, as naturally as possible, as if nothing had happened. There's probably someone waiting for you inside..." she concludes, gesturing for me to open the door.

"Who? Your sister Clara?", I ask her, a little candidly.

"Not only that. Just goof off," she insists, reproducing that gracious yet dry hand gesture inviting me to finally go into the fucking room. I translate what I understand, don't I? Lola has a bit of a temper. She's a bit impatient depending on the circumstances and directive all the time. I could be wrong, but...

"What exactly do you do?" she asks me, still in a low voice.

Okay, chief. I straighten up elegantly. I put my pants back on because they tend to sag, while smoothing out my shirt. Here, I lost a damn button in the fight with my bald man. I give Lola a discreet nod to calm her down. I rummage around, looking for the card to open the damned door. However, as I look down, I notice that the door isn't perfectly aligned. I point this out to Lola, giving her a knowing look. She replies with cautious gestures. Oh, so we have to take it easy? Okay, I understand, Lola. I'll do my best.

I push the door in front of me with all my might and it opens without resistance. The door even bounces off me once before I push it violently back against the wall again.

Lola's expression is one of rage. "Rage" clearly means: "Fuck, this is no time to show your muscles, you big asshole". Or something like that, you know. But hey, I don't care what she thinks of my muscles. I just want to get this over with and regain my composure by sipping a nice hot cup of coffee. Hell, a steaming cup of coffee is all I need.

"Who's that?" asks a voice that sounds like it's coming straight out of a voice generator. I cautiously walk over to the bed, which is empty. I motion to Lola to follow me. When she sees the empty bed, she violently grabs my arms, digging her nails into my biceps.

I move forward a little more and discover a guy, curled up in a wheelchair, tilting his head to see who's entering the room. He's standing by the unmade bed, with no trace of Clara. Who are you? What are you doing in my room?"

Shit, what a fucking smell! I've only just realized it. It stinks of containment and rust to high heaven.

"What the hell are you doing here?", I ask this shriveled guy. I don't know what ran over him, but the result is terrifying. What's more, he's drooling.

"Where are my bodyguards?" he cries through his voice generator. It makes you wonder if he didn't get it on promotion. It gives him the voice of a cartoon character.

"They're not anymore," Lola replies in a husky, menacing voice as she emerges from behind me. She digs her fingernails into my kidneys again, as if to let me know she knows this guy.

She's probably going to tell me it's her brother...

"Victor... You? Here?!" she exclaims with undisguised contempt as she strides into the room. "Did you forget your armor? Where's Clara?" she asks, inspecting every nook and cranny of the room. "And what's that unbearable smell?" she adds, covering her nose.

The generator replies, "I've been waiting for you, Lola."

All right, then. So, these two individuals know each other. He's Victor, and she's Lola. Personally, I don't really care, but I'll make a note of it. It could be useful. They may even have had an intimate relationship. I restrain my imagination so as not to take this vision of horror any further. And this smell is so nauseating. I open the window wide, causing a violent draught that rattles the front door.

A bra that was lying on the sofa flies towards Victor and clings to his head like an Alien bug trying to stick an egg in his gut. He struggles to remove it, with duck-like cries coming from his voice generator. I contemplate him for a moment, struggling in vain against this piece of cloth. He's very clumsy and lacks arm strength. Lola silently asks me to close the window while she helps Victor free himself from the bra. Pity. Yes, I think I'm feeling pity right now.

In the meantime, I'm off to the bathroom to open the small window and try to air out the place without triggering a tornado.

When I open the bathroom door, that infernal smell becomes ten times more powerful and instinctively makes me recoil.

Lola turns around and asks me, "What's wrong?"

NO TREASURE FOR THE BRAVE

I wasn't supposed to be there

Hotel Tonant bar, the day before

She's been staring at me for five long minutes already, holding my gaze persistently. Usually, I don't care too much when women give me insistent looks. They do what they want with their imagination, especially at the moment. And after all, I'm used to it. But this one, she's looking at me in a different way. As if her interest goes beyond the purely physical and sexual. No, she's not a predator looking for the best partner for her offspring, or anything like that. There's a complexity to the story her face tells. I immediately feel like an instrument in her plan.

I have to admit it confuses me, she destabilizes that cunt. I have to say I'm probably on my third or fourth drink, or maybe even more, given my state. I haven't counted.

Her face is so intense, one of those who devote their lives to a cause, no matter how small or insignificant. She's the kind of person who devotes herself body and soul to her mission, even if it's not perceived as grandiose in the eyes of others. And I'm telling you: that blonde on the other side of the bar counter, in that dilapidated hotel, is part of that stubborn tribe. The word of one who has gained an insight into human psychology between two bursts of gunfire on the battlefield.

I get lost in my thoughts. I find it hard to concentrate on an idea for long. At times, I look away, then back at her. She looks at me again and again. She's a femme fatale ready for anything. Including putting unusual pressure on me when I'm not asking for anything. I just want to relax over a drink... Well, the drink has friends...

What's his mission? What's the story behind that peculiar face? She scares me. She must be capable of making the craziest decisions to achieve her goal. She's one of those people who just won't give up.

And here I am, sitting here in front of the bar, watching this enigmatic being. I find myself imagining all sorts of scenarios in my head. Too late: I know full well that I'm in the middle of a conspiracy whose outcome still eludes me. Or perhaps this delirium exists only in my mind?

That's it: she's getting up. I hope she'll go away and leave me alone. I realize she's very tall. I'd feared it: she's coming towards me.

The mysterious woman rises gracefully from her seat, revealing a feline gait and deliciously gentle gestures in every movement. Her steps are light, almost silent. She advances with a confidence that is both elegant and intimidating. Her presence occupies the space around her. She captures the gazes of other customers. Some even dare to turn around as she passes. They can't help it. I knew it: she's a witch.

Her attire accentuates her aura of mystery. She's wearing a tight-fitting leather jacket that hugs her slim figure perfectly, giving her a bold, rebellious look. The jacket is black, worn by time. The seams seem to have withstood all the challenges the world has thrown at her.

Beneath the jacket, she sports a sky-blue shirt, whose undone buttons at the collar subtly reveal very smooth, pale skin. This touch of pastel color contrasts with the assertive character of her face and adds a certain freshness to her appearance. The shirt seems to belong to a different, less boorish world, like a vestige of her duality.

For the rough side, she wears a pair of worn jeans, marked by grease stains, as if she'd just come out of a mechanics marathon. The faded, crumpled fabric bears witness to long hours spent in out-of-the-way places. These stains tell a story of physical effort, hard work and contortions. Her jeans are a symbol. She's not here for a joke.

She approaches discreetly, almost brushing past me, before sitting down next to me.

"I know who you are. I need your help," she says without waiting, in a mysterious tone.

Oh? This enigmatic person seems to know me? Damn! "And who am I then?", I ask her with a puzzled air.

"You're the key to the treasure of the Michontas," she reveals with an expectant look, as if hoping for a reaction from me. The treasure of the Michontas... Good grief. A treasure now. I recommend a drink. I've either had too much to drink or not enough. I'm afraid she'll turn reptilian, under my misty eyes.

"Would you like something to drink?", I offer. She shakes her head, frowning, as if reprimanding me.

"Look, lady, you're lovely. But leave me out of it," I say, turning to the counter to isolate myself.

She signals the bartender to serve her the same thing I'm serving. I see. Madame likes control, and changes her mind like a weather vane.

With infinite grace, decidedly, and a sensuality I'm unprepared for, she brings her mouth close to my left ear and whispers, "If not, how would you like a hundred million?"

She straightens, a cruel smile on her lips, as if she's just stabbed me in the heart.

"A HUNDRED MILLION?", I almost scream, my eyes wide.

"Shhh... Are you an idiot, or are you doing this on purpose?" she scolds me with the expression of a stern, merciless prison guard, fearful that her secret will be divulged. Her eyes remain riveted on me, illuminated by those orange-yellow neon lights in the bar's half-light.

"No. I don't like scams. And I certainly don't like bitches like you."

She steps back on her stool, almost falling backwards. She holds onto the edge of the counter with her fingertips.

"All right. You want proof?" she asks in a tone of defiance.

"No. I don't want anything, ma'am. Try the guy on your left. You're wasting your time on me."

She observes the long-haired, white-haired old grandpa, half-asleep on his bottle, seated to her left. When her eyes land on me again, she realizes that I've discreetly slipped away and moved to the back of the room. I've almost stretched out on those old, worn but incredibly comfortable sofas. Her face becomes confused and frustrated. She stares around the room, her expression predatory and vengeful. When her gaze finally settles on my position, she stares at me with an almost frightening intensity. The bartender pours her drink, which she grabs firmly with her right hand. She stands up like a soldier at attention. With a much less graceful gait, she strides towards me. Her legs have become stiff as stilts, without the slightest suppleness in the knees.

As she approaches, I raise a glass to her health to taunt her. I'm a gambler. And above all, I don't have to take the piss. Neither does she, apparently. Once in front of me, her legs planted stiffly in a right-angled triangle, she leans towards me and pours the entire contents of her glass over my head, causing me to leap out of my seat like a spring.

"Fuck! Shit!" are the two words that escape my mouth. Yes, I'm angry. Yes, she's going to pay. Well, not yet, because she's throwing herself at me with the intention of lashing out with a series of blows, each one more disorganized than the last. I don't know where she learned to fight. In front of the mirror no doubt?

So she falls on top of me again and tries to slaughter me on the sofas. She throws a series of punches on my sides, then on my head and into my ears.

I calm her down with a brushed headbutt that turns her face toward the pale lights of the counter. I look in the same direction. The bartender and the customers have bent over to gauge our gallivanting. For a moment, they contemplate our incongruous pose on these sofas. Then they turn to go about their business. They see tougher ones every day these days.

She stands there, above me, her face lit on the side. She swallows a trickle of drool that falls on me. I feel her chest pumping air against mine. Her dangling hair caresses my ears. She's magnificent, this fury. She's just realized that I know how to hit, and to hurt. Life is unfair.

"You should never have..." she said with a growl, contorting herself like a cat bouncing on itself to regain a stable position on its paws.

She immediately falls back on me, with all her weight, and I start to feel something very unpleasant pointing towards my liver.

"Good. Are you willing to listen to me now?" she breathes breathlessly, handing me a few more drops of drool as a bonus. She's got something going on with her salivary glands. That's for sure.

With one finger, I check the area where I feel this unusual sting and discover that she's holding some kind of very sharp knife. The point is just a few millimeters away from inviting itself into my belly. This is no ordinary weapon. I can feel twists of ribbing and leather. And the blade is rough, probably rusty in places. His eyes, and his whole face, let me know that I have no interest in trying anything in this very disadvantageous position.

I contract my abs, ready to propel her body towards the coffee table adjacent to the sofa. My muscles brace, my senses alert. I launch myself with all the strength I can muster, but the blonde firmly resists, pushing me back with unexpected power. I'm thrown backwards, falling on myself in a disorderly landing.

Despite my disappointment, I waste no time. I act instinctively, handing out blind slaps like a helicopter rotor to clear the space in front of me. With each blow, I feel my anger growing, mixed with a certain frustration. However, my rage doesn't wane, I'm more precise every time. I see her in front of me, calm and satiated with slaps. She holds her sore cheeks and looks in the direction of the counter.

That's when I notice the movement around us. Customers, attracted by the commotion, have approached our impromptu street fight. They've obviously enjoyed our performance and want a second round, just for fun. They snigger amongst themselves as they slowly approach, staggering like the living dead. Their curiosity is piqued. They watch especially the blonde whose hair is dishevelled from our fight. They watch greedily. The muscular arguments of our negotiation have popped a few more buttons on the blonde's shirt, further enhancing her figure. The customers' gazes become more insistent. They really want to go further.

Not accepting this intrusion, I keep them at a distance, firmly dispersing them. Nothing and no one can disturb this moment I'm sharing with her. That's the way it is. She pisses me off, but she's my problem. And I'm not one of those people who share their problems.

Some customers, too drunk to realize their mistake, take off and run into me. Without hesitation, I push them back violently and lay them out with a few precise blows. One of them shouts: "What are you going to do? Call the police?". They all snigger with fat laughter from deep in their tired throats. They know we're all on our own. They take the opportunity to repeat this deplorable little assault three times in a row, proving that they really want to taste the forbidden fruit. Some even start undoing their belts and pulling down their pants. Yet in the end, here they are, on the ground, squirming like worms, calmed down, their eyes disoriented, satiated with blows.

The others still standing, less reckless or even more intoxicated than the previous ones, gradually submit to my tacit domination of this territory. With

a gesture, I tell them to go back to their work, silently inviting them to leave us in peace. Finally, I extend my hand to the blonde, helping her to her feet. She looks at me and thanks me. Her voice is soft and grateful, reviving my senses.

I gently guide her towards the sofas, urging her to make herself comfortable. My duty done, I'm about to take my leave, but she holds me back. Her sparkling gaze sweeps me off my feet once more.

"I need you, Oscar," she confesses with the eyes of a frightened doe. She's really ready to unroll all the chapters of the "Seduction for Dummies" manual for me tonight!

I carefully pick up the strange dagger I've just accidentally stepped on. In the silence of this part of the room, only the glow of the distant lights guides my hesitant steps towards its owner.

The metallic glint of the blade is reflected in the dark eyes of this mysterious stranger. What can I say: she's a fake blonde.

"This is yours, I believe," I said, handing her the dagger with the hilt facing her.

She grasps the unusual weapon with insolent grace and her gaze wanders over the edge of the blade to the bloody tip, like a caress. My breath catches.

A cold shiver runs down my spine as my fingers graze my belly. The wound, scarred by the vicious dagger, brings me to my senses. Carmine liquid slowly leaks from my body, reminding me that this blade could have been fatal.

A flicker of concern crosses the blonde's gaze. Does she feel remorse? Her fingers delicately brush my palm and catch a few scarlet drops, as if to steal a piece of my suffering.

The moment is suspended, frozen between pain and the unknown. An inexplicable connection is established between us. Our secrets intertwine in an intoxicating dance. The dance of emotions sweeps me away as I gaze into the eyes of this enigmatic, resourceful woman.

"Come on," she suggests, standing up and waving to follow her.

She returns to her place at the bar counter and picks up a large bag, like a country doctor's tote bag. She smiles and promises me: "My name is Clara. Let's go up to your room. I'll take care of you.

But how does she know I have a room in this hotel?

NO TREASURE FOR THE BRAVE

The harpoon

Room 618, Hotel Tonant

I enter the bathroom slowly. The horror that awaits me far exceeds my worst nightmares. The whitewashed walls of immaculate tiles now bear infamous scarlet stains, while the mirror, once a clear reflection of light, is sullied by large bloodstains. My stomach knots violently at the unbearable sight.

My gaze falls on the bathtub, filled with shredded flesh. Shock grips me as my mind grasps the horrible truth: these battered remains are Cara's remains, reduced to common shreds. Her head, previously haloed by blond curls, looms among the macabre fragments. A shiver of horror runs through my body at the extent of this abomination. In this war-torn world, I have seen things that no one should see. But those who perpetrated this cruel act, to the point of separating bone from flesh, are true monsters. I can't get used to humanity's propensity to indulge in this perverse violence. Is violence the ultimate expression of intelligence? I doubt it.

My voice echoes around the room, filled with a mixture of despair and anger: "LOLA! TA SOEUR!"

Lola immediately abandons what she's doing and rushes into the bathroom. There's a silence, which speaks volumes. Victor looks at me with the excitement of a madman. He's fidgeting, with his hands dangling near his private parts, as if he's trying to masturbate. What a staggering sight. Lola can't suppress a howl of horror and pain as she climbs out. In an impulse of love, she wanted to get closer to the bathtub, as if to hug her sister. But what was inside was too unbearable. No one could ever get used to such an atrocity. Lola screams at the top of her voice, banging her fists against the walls.

As I try to recover from this intense emotion and soothe Lola, I notice Victor, sitting in his wheelchair, brandishing a strange rod that I can't immediately identify. So that's why he was squirming frantically.

Crap! A harpoon gun!

What's he doing with that underwater hunting weapon? He's aiming at me now. His arms are shaking as if he's lifting a crushing burden. By instinct, I duck as quickly as I can and the three-pronged arrow shoots out of the speargun and into the wall, just inches from my right ear. Damn, I'd forgotten how hard these fish forks shoot! What else is this deformed guy looking for?

"OSCAR! BE CAREFUL!" cries Lola as Victor takes off to fire a second arrow in my direction. I shout to Lola for help while instinctively shielding myself: "PUSH IT!"

Without the slightest moment's hesitation, Lola sends a masterful kick into the armchair, which topples over, sending Victor tumbling. His face collides violently with the corner of the bedside table, leaving a scarlet trail in his wake. Unable to move properly, he tries to drag himself, but his weak arms won't let him move efficiently. His face is soon bathed in a pool of blood and his left eye, terribly bruised, bears witness to the violence of the impact.

I get to my feet, still confused about what's going on here. I rush to Victor's side to neutralize him completely, as he is still fidgeting as if desperate to escape.

"NO! STOP!" screams Lola, intercepting my fist intended to put an end to this diabolical hunchback.

I raise my head to her in frustration. "He just cut your sister to pieces...", I remind her, teeth clenched.

Lola lowers her face and starts to cry. She kneels down, covering her eyes with her hands.

"What have you done, you vermin? What have you done?", I growl, lifting Victor at arm's length without even realizing it. My anger increases my physical strength tenfold. Deep down, I'm ready to defy Lola's order and crack the skull of this groveling hunchback.

"Let him go! You'll kill him!" begs Lola again. I'm at a loss.

I look at Victor, struggling in my hands. She's right. I hold him firmly by his collar, squeezing his neck so hard it turns purple, a dark, ominous hue.

"Shit! Why do you want to save him?", I ask her, distraught.

Lola sighs, her face contorted by her intense crying. She knew Clara was in danger. She hadn't expected to arrive too late and discover her dead in that sinister bathtub.

"Victor saved my life...", Lola murmurs, looking at me as if imploring my understanding and forgiveness.

"That's for you to see. After all, she's not my sister."

Lola gives me an icy stare, the stare of death. I know it. But having been unable to express my violence on the cripple, I had to release it through words. I never keep negative energy inside me. We all carry within us a seed of violence just waiting to manifest itself. These words had to act as a key to unlock the hatred deep inside Lola. To give me the green light to beat Victor to a pulp.

"Leave him be. Let's go," Lola beckoned, wiping away her tears with the back of her forearm and the palm of her hand.

I stand before her like a centurion before his troops. "Are you going to leave your sister there like that?", I ask, incredulous and shocked.

Lola's accusing gaze meets mine. Her eyes convey a silent, chilling message that resonates within me: there is no proper burial today. I shiver from head to toe. The hotel staff will take care of the remains as they clean the room. They'll be careful not to alert what's left of the overwhelmed authorities.

I can see the urgency in Lola's face too, betraying the emotional chaos taking over her mind. But before I can catch up with her, she breaks into a frantic run out of the room, fleeing the carnage and her pain.

Frozen in place, my thoughts swirl in a tortuous tangle. All these thoughts paralyzed me. It left me a prisoner of myself. An uncontrollable surge of adrenaline runs through my entire being, provoking an instinctive reaction that overwhelms me. I turn abruptly and rush into the room, retracing my steps.

I brutally seize Victor and throw him against the wall with all my might. He rebounds with a crash and falls back onto the bed, leaving another trail of blood in his wake.

I'm not as mentally strong as Lola.

I couldn't keep all that hate inside me.

PAUL TOSKIAM

Echo... Solstice... Blizzard...

Lola's house

Lola slowly puts her hair back up in front of me, her gestures marked by a certain elegance. She takes her time. She's there, but she's not there. She's thinking. Each brush stroke on her hair represents a different thought. I can see it in her face, which goes from serious to happy in a second. She's thinking about everything that happened, long ago, a week ago, a day ago, today.

His once stately home is now a pile of ruins. Like a wandering soul, it stands proudly, resilient, a reminder of a glorious past, now swallowed up in the meanders of time.

In a discreet corner of the second floor, Lola has managed to set up a minimalist space where she leads a modest life. A small kitchen, barely sufficient to satisfy even the most rudimentary needs, sits alongside a micro-bathroom. A frail sofa, testimony to happy days gone by, sits timidly beside a simple table and a few creaky wooden chairs.

The place gives off an oppressive odor, mixing musty dampness with the infamous scent of mold. The walls, once covered in rich tapestries, are now shrouded in a tangible melancholy, gnawed away by time, untended. They silently mourn the decline of this once warm home.

Despite all this, Lola crosses this desolate space with disarming grace. Her eyes, imbued with a glimmer of hope, hint at an unsuspected inner strength that I have witnessed for myself. An unrivalled ability to overcome adversity. In this decrepit world, she tries to find a glimmer of humanity, an ounce of joie de vivre that will help her cope with the terrible loss of her sister Clara.

Despite Lola's unenviable situation, the time has come for me to get her to talk. Helpful by nature, I let myself be drawn into the murky affairs of this family of survivors and their illusions of lost treasures, their hopes for a better life. Yes, I know, today we're all survivors.

But the family's spirit of conquest is far removed from my immediate concerns. My life is pretty simple. The army gave me time off after I was seriously injured in an explosion. My whole back was ploughed by an explosion. And yet, I was lucky enough to receive proper care. I think of all my comrades who fell because they were not cared for on the battlefield. Since then, my life has been pretty simple, as I said. Am I hungry? I work and eat. I'm tired? I sleep. Depressed? I go for a run. I don't seek contact with others. It's easier for my mind. But I don't refuse it either. Yes, of course, like everyone else, I sometimes dream of a better future over a few drinks. But who really believes in that these days? And I know that, if those better days do come, I'll be far too old to enjoy them, even just a little. This is far from a happy state of affairs. And yet, in the eyes of some, I'm considered an optimist.

The time has come for me to really understand what Clara wanted to tell me, why she ended up dismembered and who Lola really is.

Have you ever thought about something and the person next to you suddenly started talking about it, as if by magic or telepathy? Yes ? It's amazing and disconcerting, isn't it? Well, that's exactly what Lola just did.

"Oscar. Come here. Come closer. Listen, I'm sorry. I'm sorry for everything. I'm far from perfect," she said with tenderness in her voice.

"Lola, I understand. Don't worry," I reassure her.

"There, I think it's time I gave you some explanations. You've got a right to know," she declares, sitting down beside me on the sofa, which creaks with every move we make.

I look at her, wide-eyed, a smile frozen on my face. It must be an amusing sight, because she bursts out laughing.

"What? What's wrong? Did I say something special?" she asks, intrigued.

"No, it's nothing. I was just thinking about something. Yes, I'd like to understand a little better what's going on. But I can wait while you rest. You must be emotionally drained."

"Thank you. I'm fine now. I've got to face it. No choice."

"I know. I'm the same way. Gotta keep moving."

"You're kidding me, right?". I smile. She continues, "What do you want to know?" she asks, turning a suddenly maternal gaze on me.

I look at her with squinted eyes: "Clara told me about a hundred million..."

She stares at me for a long time, almost motionless, as if trying to invent an explanation out of thin air. Her embarrassment shows clearly on her face. Then she bursts into a laugh that echoes throughout the room, reminiscent of an operatic diva. The vibrant laughter almost shakes the windows. By some miracle, they're still holding in place. I've inevitably triggered something in her. She continues to stare at me, amused, before slowly calming down.

"I see..." she finally says. "Well, my sister may have exaggerated a little."

"How much?", I ask.

"How much what?"

"If not a hundred million, then how much?"

"Oh, the money..." she searches for her words. "I don't know exactly. A lot, that's for sure. And you want me to tell you something incredible?"

"Oh, I dream about it!"

"You carry the key with you..."

"The what?"

"The key. Are you deaf?"

I stare at her, puzzled, clearly seeing that she's mocking me.

"Just relax. You're in no danger. Well, not much..." she reassures me. She gestures to me that my mouth is open and I can close it again.

"What key? The key to what?" I ask, my hands open and turned towards her, as if asking "what the fuck is this all about again?"

"The key to the treasure, Oscar. My sister gave you the key to the treasure that cost her her life."

I start frantically searching all my pockets, looking for a key. I turn over all my pockets, scanning every nook and cranny. Lola carefully observes my every meticulous move, then bursts out laughing.

Her laughter echoes through the room again, vibrant and powerful. I'm both offended by her mockery and happy to see her regain some carefree spirit.

Our phones ring frantically, abruptly shaking the atmosphere and our bodies, making the sofa squeak copiously.

Without missing a beat, Lola cried out, "Quick! Follow me!"

She leaps to her feet, rushes to the first floor and opens the old, partly battered wooden door to the basement. Her momentum is so quick that I follow instinctively, without thinking. In my haste, I catch up with her slim figure as she nearly trips over the worn stone steps. I'm careful to support her, suddenly struck by the slimness of her waistline that I hadn't noticed before.

"Lock the door!" she calls out, turning on the light and feverishly searching for candles just in case.

I take in the expanse of this large basement room with surprise. Lola has transformed this basement into a veritable refuge, equipped with everything you need to survive for a few days: weapons, tools, accessories, clothing, medical care, food and clean water. It's almost better equipped and tidier than the main floor of the house.

"What a palace!", I compliment, admiringly.

"Here, swallow this," she orders, handing me a lozenge and a small bottle of water already uncorked.

"Crap. You got any Boréale?"

Stammering these words, I show a mixture of surprise and excitement.

She nods, letting me know that I should consume it right away. I ponder. I've never tried this before. I've heard it causes powerful hallucinations. Gigantic hallucinations, hence the name. However, I sometimes eat contraband meat, not caring whether it comes from a dog or a horse. She promptly gobbles up her lozenge. She beckons me with her eyes to do the same as she greedily gulps down half a bottle of water, as if she's just come out of a thirsty desert crossing. I decide to do the same, imitating her gestures. A smile forms on her lips.

"This is no time for jokes," she says, cranking up the radio. She plugs a cable above it, presumably the antenna to the outside, and turns it on. Soft music, covered by crackling noises, fills the apartment-sized space.

"It smells great in here. Is the air filtered?", I ask.

She then points out two air vents and explains that the facility is equipped with air filters and mechanical back-up air conditioners. She seems to have thought of everything. It's better equipped than most of the military camps I've been to in the last two years.

What I thought was a dark animal skin hanging elegantly on the vast, uncluttered wall, turns out to be far more extraordinary. My astonished eyes gaze upon an ancient map, a veritable treasure trove from the days when navigators dared to face the unknown of unexplored lands. A relic from the time when the Earth was flat...

Amused by my amazement, Lola approaches me in front of the map. Her attitude betrays a discreet, almost mysterious pride, as if she held a thousand-year-old secret in her hands.

"Do you like it?" she murmurs indifferently, pretending not to care. A simple ornament, she makes

me understand with a vague hand gesture. Is it really? My mind struggles to accept such a banal explanation, in stark contrast to the magic that emanates from this piece, which looks so much like an original. It must be this piece of old paper that's worth a hundred million!

Carefully unfolded along the length of the wall, the map reveals its ancient contours, its delicate hues bearing witness to centuries gone by. The intricate details, meticulously traced, reveal a world still in search of discovery and wonder. Unable to contain my astonishment, I realize that I've only scratched the surface of Lola's personality. An insatiable, implacable certainty dawns on me: it's high time to get out the drill.

I exclaim loudly, proud of my discovery: "It's the treasure map!"

Lola gives me an amused look and shrugs her shoulders.

"Bingo! Captain Obvious found it!" she congratulates me, raising her eyes to the ceiling in despair and "is he kidding or is he a real jerk?"

A thud approaches our position. Now I'm thinking like a soldier again. I know that roar by heart.

"Tanks!" murmurs Lola, ducking into a corner of the large room as if the ceiling were about to collapse in on us.

She beckons me to join her. I go immediately, without hesitation. We're hidden away, pressed up against this darker corner, leaning against two walls at right angles. Her body shudders slightly, betraying a palpable apprehension. In this stifling basement, the heat is overwhelming. It's not the temperature that makes her shiver, it's the fear that runs through her being. Her eyes slowly scan the ceiling, searching for answers in the cracks that run through it, as the menacing rumble progresses above us. It's not just a rumble, it's an unimaginable force advancing, crushing everything in its path. Before long, the foundations of the house are shaking. Floor, ceiling, walls, furniture - everything is shaken by this insidious seismic wave. The vibrating din grips our chests, compressing our eardrums too. Lola beckons me to chew, a gesture familiar to her. She knows exactly what it means.

My left wrist hurts more and more. I realize she's dug her nails into it. Being left-handed, I'm not too happy about this.

"Fifty-three armored vehicles...North-Northwest...Support drones...Laser scanning...Constant speed...Progress complete in twenty-four minutes...Echo...Solstice...Blizzard...Repeat...Echo...Solstice...Blizzard...", announces the radio in a tangle of sizzle of all kinds.

My heart starts pounding in my chest. Lola is gradually falling prey to indescribable terror, and I hold her tightly in my arms, desperately trying to bring her some comfort. But her tremors become more and more violent, and soon she begins to moan, then to cry. Her sobs echo through the room, jerky and heartbreaking.

I feel her whole body vibrate under my hands, as if this episode had awakened some terrible pain buried inside her for too long, a trauma she'd been holding inside her, lurking in the dark recesses of her mind. Her body reacts, agitated by uncontrollable spasms, as if trying to expel the unbearable visions assailing her. Her eyes burn with tears, and their erratic movements give the impression that she is daydreaming, as if possessed. She contorts her body, her face twists in pain. Her body arches back. I hold her to me with all my strength, fearing that in this panic attack, she'll hurt herself against the walls of the room.

Her breathing becomes ragged, her mouth open, desperately searching for air. Gradually, the trembling subsides. Her breathing becomes calmer. At last, her eyes meet mine. She's exhausted, covered in sweat, her hair soaked and sticking to her face. She gradually comes to her senses, scanning the room as if discovering it for the first time. Gently, I release her from my embrace, giving her a little space to relax and breathe.

I hand her a second small bottle of water, hoping to refresh her. At first, she weakly pushes it away, but eventually grabs it with both hands, emptying it in one gulp without even taking a breath. I grab a piece of paper towel and carefully wipe away the sweat dripping down her forehead, absorbing every drop that threatened to run into her eyes.

"Thank you," she says suddenly, squeezing my wrists with surprising force, almost to the point of breaking them. My left one hurts like hell. Her voice trembles, and her eyes still reflect the terror she has just experienced.

With the pressure off, she seeks refuge against me and, relaxing all her muscles, falls asleep in my arms. I gaze at her. She looks a lot like Clara. I feel like I'm reliving something. Her peaceful, abandoned face finally calms me too. I fall asleep beside her.

I dream of the northern lights.

NO TREASURE FOR THE BRAVE

Reparing Victor

Clinique du Dr Berthold

Victor is still breathing. It's a miracle. He was kept alive with the utmost care from the hotel room to the clinic run by Dr. Berthold, a good friend.

Victor's empty gaze is locked in on himself. He seems to be a prisoner in his own body. A thin layer of sweat beads on his forehead, testifying to the deep distress in which he finds himself. The oppressive silence of the room is interrupted only by the steady rhythm of his jerky, wheezing breath.

"Is he still alive?" asks Berthold as he storms into the operating room.

"Yes. He's a fascinating specimen, Doctor..." replies Sofia, his nurse.

Berthold observes Victor gravely, his eyebrows furrowing in concern. He is aware of the weight of his responsibility, knowing that without his intervention, Victor will remain forever trapped in his condition, unable to return to a bearable life. He also knows who he's dealing with. Victor isn't the first person to come along. There are a dozen not exactly friendly types lurking outside the operating room door. Dr. Berthold doesn't like being watched so closely. But then, he's known Victor for a long time and has already "fixed" him on numerous occasions. He smiles inwardly. Every time he sees Victor again, he's in an even worse state of disrepair than the last time. Life as a bandit leaves its mark. Those are Victor's men at the door. They picked him up in extremis, lifeless in a room at the Hotel Tonant downtown.

As he leaned closer, terror overcame the surgeon. He's rarely seen such a mutilated body still alive. And he knows he can't miss, or this operation may well be his last.

But Berthold has no qualms. He loves money. He takes a deep breath, wiggling his gloved fingers, and slowly approaches Victor.

The operating room is plunged into semi-darkness. The sterile white walls seem to close in on themselves like a shell, while the surgical instruments emit a cold, sinister glow in a concert of small, regular clicks and clanks. The surgery Berthold is about to perform resembles a danse macabre, where every gesture is of the utmost importance.

At this moment, Berthold knows he is this poor cripple's last hope. This heavy responsibility weighing on his shoulders oppresses him more than he thought. It's also the moment for him to display his immense talent as the city's most renowned war surgeon.

He glances at the medical team around him... No, it's an old reflex from the days when he still practiced in acceptable conditions. His team for the day consists of Sofia, who is as attentive and dedicated as ever. Berthold and Sofia are ready to erase the traces of Victor's mistreatment, to offer him a new chance, an extension. But do they really have a choice?

Berthold leans towards Victor again and offers him a few words of encouragement, hoping to ease his anxieties and instill a little strength. He promises that all will be well, that soon he'll be free of this unbearable prison, that his body will regain some semblance of mobility. Victor stares at the surgeon without really seeing him, his bloodshot eyes reflecting an immense sadness.

The tension rises a notch as Berthold begins to prepare his equipment. Each instrument is manipulated with maniacal precision, while Victor's heartbeat almost echoes in the silence of the operating room. The minutes tick by. A leaden silence envelops the room, with only the sound of bated breath to be heard. The doctor's hands are slightly clammy in his gloves, but his mind is clear and focused. He realizes that every moment counts and could be fatal. He must act without delay.

The scalpel, assisted by a mechanical arm, glides with unprecedented precision over Victor's skin, beginning the process of opening up his body. The silence is broken by the sound of surgical instruments mingling with the patient's jerky breathing. Berthold is absorbed in his work, his flawless technique testifying to his experience and expertise. Victor's men watch with interest the doctor's precise movements, each in turn, through the round glass in the door. He doesn't like to operate raw: with the patient conscious. This was an express request from Victor's men. They didn't want general anesthesia, which they felt was too risky. Berthold disagreed. But no one cares about his opinion in these circumstances. He's become accustomed to yielding to the arguments of a gun pointed at his temple. He knows he won't save medicine. He's content to save one patient at a time.

The intensity rises again when Berthold reaches the most critical part of the operation. His heart races as he attempts to navigate around the obstacles in his path. A drop of sweat slides down his forehead, then a trickle of drops. He doesn't dare ask Sofia to sponge it off, for fear of losing concentration and committing the irreparable. Sofia tries to sponge his forehead, but he refuses with a shake of his head.

The psychological terror that grips Victor seems contagious, as if it's spreading to everyone around him. Berthold and Sofia's eyes are riveted on their patient, their concentration absolute, their fear in their bellies.

"Is everything going as agreed?" asks one of Victor's men as he enters the operating room.

Berthold gives him a terrible look and asks not to be interrupted again: Victor's survival depends on it. Surprisingly, his wishes are respected. Victor is a precious asset to his men. He must have promised them something very special for them to take such good care of him. Berthold senses this. He knows bandit gangs, cruel and savage, even to their leaders. In these troubled times, this particular clientele represents a significant part of his business. Morally, he disapproves. Financially, they pay cash.

The hours fly by. After these intense, sustained efforts, Berthold managed to partially straighten Victor's body. His spine has been badly damaged, probably by a terrible impact against a wall or the ground during a fall. With Sofia, he carefully places him on the stretcher that will take him to the recovery room, where he will be monitored for the next few hours. The worst is behind them. Victor is saved. Berthold and Sofia are saved.

Berthold meticulously closes Victor's body, suturing every opening with the utmost care. The room fills with life again. Even the medical machines seem to greet this return to normal with their multiple crackling sounds. Berthold and Lola exchange a few looks of complicity, aware of the miracle that has just happened, and how lucky they were. That little pinch of luck without which life can disappear.

Victor is finally physically free. However, the mental consequences of his accident have yet to be assessed. Berthold knows that this is just one step in Victor's long battle to regain his original health. He beckons through the glass door of the operating theatre to the two men standing in front. They enter and, in their own way, examine their boss's body. Their gloved fingers explore the scars, like a butcher working his quarter of meat.

"Did you find anything, Doctor? Anything unusual?" one of the men asks.

Berthold takes off his gloves and stares at them. He knows they're looking for something very special, and that Victor's body would be worthless if they found it.

"No," Berthold said blasély. "Victor's as good as new. Finally... You can pick him up in three or four hours. My work is done," adds Berthold, holding out his open hand to demand payment.

One of the two men smiles at him, amused, then snaps his fingers. The second man leaves the room for a few seconds and returns with a briefcase, which he hands to Berthold.

"The count's good," says the first man, pointing to the briefcase Berthold hands to Lola. She opens it and begins to mentally count the number of small packages in which small gold bars are carefully wrapped.

Victor's life is worth a lot, a lot of money.

NO TREASURE FOR THE BRAVE

After the storm

Lola's house

"Can you see her?" asks Lola, gently lifting my cheek in front of the bathroom mirror. Frankly, she's got a knack for sticking her fingers in my mouth with such ease... Does she think she's at home? Basically, she lifts my cheek as if I were her docile little dog. It's probably because she feels that part of what's there belongs to her. I've become her partial property.

I frown, carefully examining my open mouth. "No, I don't see anything special," I confess, slightly disconcerted.

Lola lets out a frustrated sigh, then moves her finger in front of my eyes for me to follow carefully. "Look closely, here..." she insists.

From my angle of view, I finally make out a fine engraving in black ink on my tooth. How the fuck did I miss this? It's like discovering a second nose in the middle of my forehead. The thing that was there, but completely overlooked. The beauty of this realization suddenly overwhelms me. "Ah, yes... that's it... shit, what's that?", I exclaim, confused and worried.

Lola nods confidently, delighted that I'm finally joining her reality. "I told you: it's the key," she asserts with an undeniable conviction that fascinates me.

"I have to hand it to your sister, she was an artist. She drew all that stuff while I was sleeping? With all those details? All those intricate little lines and flourishes?"

I step away from the mirror, leaving wisps of mist on it. I turn to Lola, trying to read the emotions on her face as best I can. "Honestly, do you want my opinion?", I ask her.

She's already scrutinizing me with some suspicion, anticipating my words. "Yes, go ahead, I'm listening," she replies, slightly defensive.

"I think you're all nuts in your family," I blurt with amusement and aplomb.

Lola squints, a wry smile at the corner of her lips. She seems almost pleased, as if she's been waiting for this remark all along.

"So if I summarize," I say, "Without asking my opinion, your sister kidnaps me - sort of - then she puts me to sleep, and rapes me if it turns out? Then she takes out her equipment, her kind of portable dental practice I imagine? And then, bang! she tattoos some kind of hieroglyphic or secret code on my tooth! A healthy tooth at that!" I catch my breath and continue: "And now I'm supposed to follow you and trust you? To open the door to I don't know what hypothetical treasure? The location of which only a madman knows? Is that it? A madman, a perverted old man with whom you have a very unhealthy relationship, even though he's only ever wanted one thing: to fuck you. Have I got this right? Did I get it right?" I finish, breathless, and with a strong desire to rewind time to avoid that disturbing witch tattoo.

She stares at me, impassive. "Yes, that's about it," she finishes thoughtfully, without trying to contradict me, even though I'd been waiting for that.

"That's it? Anyway, you don't care what I think, do you?"

"No. Stop it with that. It's a biological key. The tooth is just a simple way of keeping it active without risking losing the key. I know, it's stupid, but it's all we've found. At least you see, it's reliable. So you can't lose it or have it stolen. Well, most of the time, I mean. You can usually tell if someone wants to pull a tooth, can't you?" she explains, miming the pulling of a tooth, which she then pretends to throw over her shoulder to make me smile.

"I don't know. I did get the tooth tattooed without realizing it, so the rest...", I conclude, dubiously.

She invites me to approach the large map hanging on the wall.

"See this ancient map that fascinates you so much? Well, there's a treasure inside..." she murmurs, with a grand, enigmatic gesture, overplaying the splendor of the work and the suspense.

Our eyes meet, creating a palpable tension between us. "You mean... in the paper of the card?".

She stares at me, silent, arms crossed, as if I've just turned into a clown. A cheap version at that. Then she bursts out laughing, unabashedly, as she's so good at doing. "No, silly. This map shows you the Maliscera region in the south," she retorts, her tone still mocking.

"And?"

"Well, that's where the treasure is... The treasure of the Michontas," she declares confidently and eruditely.

"Michontas... don't know... Wait... I'm there. Michontas... The Michontas... Clara told me about them. That's it, I remember!", I shout, in a shower of happiness at having rediscovered this memory.

"Congratulations," comments Lola, admiring my dance of happiness made up of little tremors all over my body and a masterful stretch, as if I were rising from my own grave.

"And who are these Michontas? Traders?" I ask, mischievously, but dreading a lecture on anthropology.

"We don't know yet. It's a recent discovery. The conquistadors crossed their path, and..."

"Stop! Say no more. The Michontas have bitten!"

She shrugs and continues: "This card was found by my father, Adrien," she continues, eager to focus me on her family history, while my whole being reminds her that I don't give a damn.

"Adrien? Is he an archaeologist?", I ask, to feign interest.

"Art dealer. He died during the first invasion."

"Shit. Sorry...", I sympathize, to feign a shred of humanity.

"We've all lost at least someone..." she comments, lowering her eyes.

"That's true. Okay, so that's why you need me?", I ask, puzzled.

"Yes," she replies, staring at me intently, with that famous locking gaze she's used on me since the first moments we met. Like her sister Clara, Lola doesn't let go of her prey and holds me by an invisible leash.

"But why did Clara carve that thing on my tooth?"

"And why not?"

"I mean, she could have just given me a drawing, right? Or a photo? Or given it to you directly?", I question, still a little more puzzled, even suspicious.

With an air of growing anger, Lola replies: "It's not as simple as you describe... Victor has been watching us for a few weeks. And he's just stepped up the hunt. He's on the case and he's not going to give up."

"Tell me anyway. At this point, I think I can swallow anything. Tell me why she didn't tattoo it on one of her own teeth that 'biological' key? Tell me why your sister decided to fuck with me about it?", I ask, sure I'm winning the point.

"Oscar, you ask too much of me. I'm not Clara. She's the one who held the key. All I know is that she felt in danger. When Victor bought the coordinates of this treasure on the encrypted networks, he went crazy. He immediately realized that he'd stumbled upon what could be the hit of a lifetime. That's how we saw him again, after all these years. He chased us home. He discovered these coordinates among a batch of old objects that belonged to my father. He tracked Adrien's every move. No doubt obsessively and vindictively at first. He got it illegally, of course. And since Dad's death, Victor has begun an even more thorough investigation. He put a lot of resources on the table. The coordinates were encrypted on an extremely ancient parchment that described an incredibly rich treasure. The kind of document everyone wants to find once in their life, especially people like Victor. He had probably visited this treasure before, but had not been able to access it. He realized he was missing something essential."

"The key."

"Bingo!"

"And this treasure, where is it on the map?", I question, insisting on each word.

"Ah, you see? Money, always money...", she murmurs, a touch sarcastically.

"It's okay, it's not even funny. I'm not the scavenger you think I am. Okay, where is it?", I ask, impatient for a straight answer.

"Well, I'd say I don't know," she reveals, which finishes me off.

I act like I'm going to give up and walk away, taking the tattooed tooth with me. In short, I sulk.

"The worst part is, I'm not kidding. I've got an idea, but I'm not going to rake the whole map with a metal detector am I?"

"And why not? The most basic methods often produce extraordinary results..."

"No, no. You've got the card in front of you: go ahead!" she taunts me, sure of her point.

"And what's this idea you have?"

"No, no. It's too vague to talk about."

"Hello confidence! Are we a team or enemies?"

"You're complicating things too much, Oscar. I'm about to find out. And I'm keeping you out of it to protect you. You're involved enough as it is."

I appreciate that. What a nice attempt to win me over. It must work often, since she still uses that ruse.

"You're playing with my nerves, Lola. First, your sister - rest her soul - and now you?", I mumble, trying to soothe the anger that's rising up inside me and giving me the urge to... you know what. You have to know how to channel in life.

"Well, finally, I have my little theory. By deduction, I think I've identified the town, well, the village: Lonesso. And the only buildings that could contain such a vestige. But Victor knows. He knows the exact latitude and longitude," she adds with a hint of defiance in her voice.

I freeze, my eyes wide, unable to find the words to express my dismay. Oh my God... Wait, wait, you're not going to tell me that...", I stammer before realizing that it's all going to start all over again.

"Yes, I am. And he's going to want us back," she confirms, accentuating the turmoil invading my mind.

"Fucking hell...", I said, trying to keep my composure despite my growing panic. I hadn't really realized that, according to her, this guy can come back from the dead. "But I smashed him against the bedroom wall on the way out. I didn't tell you because I didn't want to add anger to your grief. You see, I wanted to protect you too," I said, a hint of mischievous mockery in my voice.

"Very funny," she congratulates me on my pirouette. "Don't worry, Victor always comes back. He's been known to do that. It's a parameter I've taken on board," Lola reveals, in a voice that's both dark and enigmatic. "He's going to want to find us. And we'll be waiting for him..." she adds, crossing her arms again, legs slightly apart to lower her center of gravity. She continues, "And this time, I won't hold you back!"

"And you couldn't find those coordinates before?"

"No. Apart from my father, no one knew of the existence of this parchment and map. Clara and I simply discovered this key among the unlikely chaos of his belongings. We spent months trying to understand the true meaning of this object and to make the connection with a probable location. Now that we've made the connection, everything seems obvious, in hindsight. But it took us a long time. If it hadn't been for his friends and former colleagues, we'd never have made it."

"Damn. It's so beautiful I almost want to believe it."

"Well, it doesn't make any difference to you. You're just the keyholder today."

"Your natural sympathy is getting the better of you..."

"It runs in the family. Haven't you ever wondered why Clara chose you?"

"Uh... I've got a pretty good idea, though."

"Well, it's not that idea," she affirms, amused by my wide-open eyes. She continues in a tone of confidence: "I'm sorry to disappoint you. She chose you because you were there, in that bar, at that moment."

"No shit?"

"Oh, she must have reckoned you were about the only one around the counter capable of surviving the time it took to be able to use the key."

I stand there without a word, admiring Lola's wild beauty. Adversity can destroy you, but it can also reveal you.

Well aware of the impact she's beginning to have on me, Lola suggests I follow her out of the basement, out of the house. She's no fool. She knows exactly what she's doing. She knows I've taken on too much all at once, and that I need a break, some fresh air.

As we make our way along the front of the house, we discover the devastation wrought by the tank unit that passed close by. The vegetation, crushed and blackened, was instantly consumed by a relentless fire. A few wisps of smoke still billow here and there, silent witnesses to the radiant heat.

"What about that old lady who wanted to take me I don't know where?", I ask, remembering that episode when my mind was still asleep. I'm not a morning person.

"Victor..." she murmurs, lost in thought.

"Who the fuck is Victor anyway?", I ask as I stop walking. "I feel like he's controlling your life, and has been for a long time. Am I wrong?"

I'm desperate to understand the sequence of events. They all know each other? But they're willing to destroy each other for money? A normal family circle.

Silently, she continues her walk, finally stopping at a precise spot in front of the house. I watch her as she searches for something on the ground, with precise, methodical gestures. Crouching down, she clears away the heaped-up brown earth to reveal a large stone that emerges slightly from the ground, evoking the bald skull of a buried giant. She points her index finger at the stone slab.

"Do you see that stone sticking out of the ground?" she asks gravely.

I gently drop to my knees, facing her from the other side, facing her. My eyes rest curiously on the mysterious stone that so attracts her attention. She pulls her hair up and tucks it behind her ears.

"What is it?", I ask in a voice laced with curiosity, my words rising softly in the air heavy with mystery that surrounds us. No, I'm just kidding. The air isn't heavy and I don't care about its mystery. I'm sorry about that. I try but my mind wanders again. I find it hard to concentrate on one subject for long.

She looks at me, her face slightly veiled by the shadow of a cloud that has just hidden the sun. The wind gently caresses her hair, and loosens it from behind her ears, making it fall limply after playing with it. As you can see, my mind clings to anything: it lives its life.

"This is where Victor fell," she reveals in a soft, secretive voice, almost as if afraid of awakening spirits from the past. Her furtive glances at the ground betray a certain emotion, which soon overwhelms her. She carefully clears away the rest of the earth that has piled up on the stone, like an archaeologist on a fragile relic.

I remain silent for a moment. Did Victor fall on it? The image takes shape in my mind. It imposes itself on me.

"Victor fell on it?", I vocalize my first hunch, out of who knows where, and unaware of the emotional impact of my words.

She straightens abruptly, a glint of anger burning in her eyes, contrasting with the angelic beauty of her face. Her sudden sharp movements reveal her displeasure at my reaction. A feeling of surprise, almost rejection, takes hold of her.

"You just don't get it, do you?" she snaps, her voice echoing in the air, carried on the wind.

I watch her walk away, her sulky mood painted on her face. "Listen to me, you little cunt. I wanted to avenge your sister. Twice I risked my life for you. So please, go lecture someone else. Please."

I take a few moments to think. Finally, I add: "Look, Lola, I think I've seen enough. All you have to do is take a photo of my tooth, or scan it, do what you like. Then you'll have your key. And I'm done with your stories. We're even. You can keep your treasure."

She turns abruptly back to me, her eyes filled with unexpected sadness. This time, she looks at me like a child abandoned by the side of the road because there's no more food to feed her, condemned to wander alone.

There's no doubt about it: Lola is an outstanding actress.

NO TREASURE FOR THE BRAVE

The carcass

Victor's men stand on alert around his bed, watching for any sign that their leader has woken up. The bunker is bathed in dim but sufficient light, creating a serene and reassuring atmosphere.

Mutaff, Victor's right-hand man, leans over him, scrutinizing his weakened body. He waits, aware that the future of their mission depends on Victor's successful convalescence. Finally, Victor's eyelids open, revealing highly mobile eyes that scrutinize every corner of the room.

Victor struggles to get to his feet. His hand trembles on the edge of the bed, seeking invisible support. His body refuses to cooperate, causing him to fall back heavily onto the bed. A glance around him reveals his men, each worried face a reminder of his broken condition.

Suddenly, a brutal anger overcomes him, his voice echoing through the bunker like a thunderstorm. He hates this feeling of being a beast in a creek, unable to get up, unable to move. He rants and raves, his breathing quickening, as if he's running out of air.

Mutaff advances slowly towards Victor, speaking softly to soothe his anger. "The armor is ready," he informs, his voice becoming almost a whisper. Mutaff suggests that this armor is the only solution to regaining relaxed mobility. The idea of putting on his combat armor repulses Victor. He'd hoped he'd be able to get away with it this time without having to reconnect with that second skin, laden with so many bad memories.

But Mutaff insists. He knows the armor is necessary for their mission. The treasure won't wait, and Victor will need all his physical faculties to succeed. Mutaff deftly enumerates his arguments, even though he knows he's raising Victor's ire. And he knows that Victor's anger can be fatal.

Mutaff

's uncompromising attitude triggers a conflict in Victor, whose thoughts race between the shame of being so dependent on that cursed armor, and the imperious call of the treasure. He must make a choice: listen to his pride, which commands him to refuse, or follow the voice of reason and reclaim this coveted treasure. But is Victor reasonable?

Victor's men form a circle around him, slumped on his bed. He can see their accusing stares. This band of mercenaries is not here by chance, nor to keep him company. Their suspicious eyes meet, like wolves sizing each other up.

"All right...", Victor lets out in a grumble, barely raising his hand in a gesture of submission and fatality.

With a snap of his fingers, Mutaff calls for the pedestal supporting the imposing armor to be moved forward, which immediately makes a majestic entrance into the room, gliding silently and precisely under the synchronized thrust of two men.

Victor gives Mutaff

a prickly, impatient look, insisting that he clear the room. Victor has complexes. More than anything else in the world, he doesn't want his men to witness the pathetic spectacle of his deformed body trying to climb into this gigantic carcass.

On Mutaff's orders, the room emptied in a matter of seconds. He then carefully approaches the articulated crane that will lift Victor's still-sore body and hoist him into his armor.

Victor stares at her, silent. "Closer..." he asks with a gesture of his left arm, which undulates in the air like a belly-dancing snake.

PAUL TOSKIAM

The guardian angel

Deserted street, in the past

Lola was trapped by a gang of thugs who wanted to make some easy money, have some fun, and why not shoot a few nice videos. They had waited for her outside her school and dragged her here. This little, poorly-lit street fit the bill perfectly: little light, the occasional stray passer-by, no cameras. It was one of the best blind spots in town.

They beat Lola mercilessly and threatened to inflict an even worse fate on her. They weren't after her personally. They wanted her father Adrien's money. At least some of his money. Lately, he'd been parading his ostentatious success as an international art dealer a little too much on professional social networks: his best sales, his best finds, his celebrations in small groups in places each more luxurious than the next. Inevitably, he gained visibility. Any kind of visibility.

This gang of fun-loving youngsters didn't have to think long before deciding that Adrien had a head for paying good money to find his daughter. With his side parting and otherworldly tailored suits, he had all the trappings of a good target. An easy target. But hitting him directly wouldn't be as profitable as hitting his beloved daughter.

This wasn't the first time these young assailants had tried their hand at this. They already had a few victims to their credit and a booty that was growing by the minute. Without having to force their talent, they had found the loophole to lose the cautious, gentrified forces of law and order. In addition to this weak resistance from law enforcement, they also had no fear of the justice system, which had become obese and ideological. All this they had assimilated and incorporated into their operations. They knew how to make the most of it. Despite their youth, they were a crime start-up with exponential and formidable growth

71

potential. They knew how to maximize their actions. In their minds, crime was a business like any other. They were the new vermin without soul, morals or law, and this era gave them carte blanche.

Before getting the father to pay, the plan was to enjoy his daughter's charms a little - a lot - in their own way. As Lola tried and failed to cry out for help, struggling, frightened and desperate, an unexpected man appeared around the corner. It was Victor, once Adrien's best friend.

Victor, scarred by the memory of Adrien's betrayal, now lived in a wheelchair. Nevertheless, despite his physical pain and broken heart, he had chosen to transcend his resentment to help Lola. Violence and night had become his companions. It was into this merciless universe that he threw himself to protect the woman he had sworn to protect since birth. His huddled figure was that of a man weakened, almost broken, by the trials he had endured. His face was marked by pain and sadness. His wrinkles bore witness to the burdens he had borne. He was broken, but still alive. Victor was a survivor, in the truest sense of the word.

That day, his whole body exuded fragility, wrapped in a worn jacket and clothes he seemed to have been wearing for weeks without changing. His hands were unresponsive. They had long since lost their suppleness. He clutched them tightly to the worn armrests of his armchair, like a last bulwark against the outside world.

And yet, despite this fragile appearance, his silhouette, strangely menacing, was almost frightening, like a supernatural apparition: that of a silent, implacable guardian. As his silhouette stood out against the backdrop of the street, he exuded an inexplicable strength: that of a man who has chosen to overcome his own suffering in order to help.

Every movement he made was as clumsy as it was calculated. Every clumsy movement of his hands bore witness to an unshakeable will to protect and save. His strength lay in his desire for justice, to defend

Lola, at all costs, against the dark forces that surrounded him on this cursed street. Against the sons of bitches who were plaguing the city.

A breath of conquest accompanied her rickety wheelchair as it moved ineluctably towards the gang ready to perpetrate the unspeakable. His face distorted by his rage to conquer, Victor had forgotten that fear even existed. That nagging fear that burned inside him, consuming him a little more every day. He never really recovered from his accident: not in body, not in soul. Yet this time, he felt an unshakeable strength propelling him towards a new destiny, as if he'd found in his crippled condition an unsuspected power. Or was it just the courage of unconsciousness?

Like an avenging angel, Victor nonetheless decimated the criminals one by one, eliminating their malevolent presence. With his means, with his trembling hands, with his brand-new ardor, he had planted them all with his harpoon-rifle, reloading the arrows one after the other, methodically. His violence was unprecedented. Each blow was a declaration to the universe, a way of saying that light always triumphs over darkness. Clearly, he was forcefully expelling something dark from his being. Sweat beaded on his forehead, mingled with invisible tears, betraying his physical pain and emotional burden. But he ignored this suffering to protect Lola. Like all those who had to live the rest of their lives diminished, Victor had developed a whole arsenal of techniques and tricks to compensate for his handicap. There was

nothing perfect about it. But he surprised himself with his new-found combat efficiency.

As the thugs fell, Lola gradually regained the hope that had been erased by the violence. She watched Victor with admiration, feeling security return to her heart and envelop her like a gentle embrace. At that very moment, Victor was much more than a protective presence. He had become a hero, a savior who had stepped out of the shadows to save Lola's life. To give her back a life, an existence free of terror.

When the last of the gang fell to the ground, pierced through and through, Victor, exhausted but proud, rolled towards Lola like a duck gliding over water. His gaze, charged with infinite tenderness, met Lola's. They both knew that their friendship was over. They both knew that their bond, forged by tragedy and trust, was now indestructible.

NO TREASURE FOR THE BRAVE

The right location

Village of Lonesso, Maliscera region

"According to my calculations, there are two possibilities left," Lola shows me over a photo of the map on her phone. "That bank you see there...", she points her index finger at a storefront with a few half-ruined columns, "... or that church", she points me to the remains of an old building whose steeple and roof have been torpedoed, probably several times.

"Really? How can you be sure?"

"If I knew that, we'd already be there, you idiot!" she throws at me with a shrug.

"So we're going to wait for the other cripple to show up?"

Silence.

"And depending on where it's headed we'll know where the treasure is?", I scoff.

"You catch on fast. That's good," she taunts me, pointing to a slowly approaching armored vehicle kicking up brown dust in this desolate village.

Lonesso, once typical of the region and long a haven for its golden youth, has been reduced to a pile of ruins and rubble by a series of brutal attacks. The main street is ripped up, covered with gaping cracks and craters left by the explosions. The buildings, once proud and welcoming, are now dilapidated, their walls ripped open and their windows shattered. The facades, scarred by the passage of time and battle, seem to be struggling to stay upright.

In places, vegetation has even begun to reclaim its rights over the concrete, popping up from every crack and crevice. Weeds and creepers stretch along the walls, giving the whole a dark, suffocating appearance.

Trees, once carefully tended, now stand twisted and deformed. Their bare branches reach like skeletal fingers to the sky, like a prayer that all this will soon end.

Silence, interrupted only by the sound of the wind and the distant echoes of a nearby weapons factory, reigns supreme. The few remaining inhabitants blend into the scenery like shadows, burrowing into dark corners to escape prying eyes.

Lonesso has become an abandoned world, where the scars of war have replaced life.

We hid in one of the buildings, which has lost part of its facade and all its windows. It offers a full, direct view of the square. I look through the binoculars to pick out the details of the vehicle and identify its crew.

"Fuck...", I almost scream as I see something incredible inside, and hard to describe.

"What is it?" asks Lola, taking the binoculars from me.

She concentrates, adjusts the knob and comments in turn: "Shit... We're in trouble..."

"It's ugly, isn't it?"

"Yes. He's put on his armor," Lola explains to me with her eyes wide open.

"And?"

"Don't be impatient, you'll find out soon enough," she informs me as she moves to the other window closer to the vehicle, to confirm the contents of the armored car that has just stopped in front of the bank.

"It's the bank!", I shout excitedly.

She takes her eyes off the binoculars, turns her head to me and says, "You should scream louder. I don't think they heard you properly..."

I remain silent and blush. Well, I don't know. In any case, I feel a wave of heat flood my whole body and my armpits are sweating profusely.

The metallic clang of the armoured hatch echoes in the silence below. The few passers-by in the vicinity move away and hide, but to get a better look. Like me, they're curious to discover what's hidden inside this imposing war machine.

I pick up the binoculars again to get a better feel for the scene.

"Hey, don't you know how to ask for things? Normally?" she grumbles after my curt gesture. I choose to ignore her. The show downstairs is too absorbing.

An armed man with an imposing build slowly emerges from the armored car. His piercing gaze, concealed behind combat goggles, immediately creates a palpable sense of tension.

"Do you know this one?"

Lola doesn't answer.

"Hey, do you know him?"

Still no answer. She looks off into the distance, as if we have a clear view of the ocean. I get angry: "Fuck, this isn't the time, Lola! Who is this guy?"

She flinches and gives me a murderous look: "It's Mutaff, how's that?"

"Not at all no. Who's Mutaff?"

"It's Victor's toy. Or something, you know?"

"Yes, I see, well... I imagine..."

With confident steps, Mutaff heads for the buildings opposite the armored car.

"What's he like?" she asks.

"He's dressed all in black and brown leather, emphasizing a rugged yet elegant look to his outfit. His ensemble includes a black leather jacket, fastened with shiny metal buttons, and brown leather pants of impeccable quality."

Lola suddenly bursts out laughing, so hard that she lets out a salvo of little jerky hyena cries. "Hey, I wasn't asking you for the commentary on a fashion show," she jokes, trying as hard as she can to hold back so as not to draw attention to ourselves, but to no avail. "I just wanted to know if he was aggressive or calm, you know? That sort of thing..." she clarifies, continuing to laugh herself to tears, mouth wide open.

A little frustrated, I continue, "He wears black and brown leather sheaths that girdle his chest crosswise... They're filled with ammunition. Lots and lots of ammo."

"Really?" she laughs again. "Let me see!" she demands, snatching the binoculars out of my hands.

"Ah, I see, you're right. It's nice. I like his cowboy hat, too. And his high boots over his pants, and pointy too! No, frankly, the guy's hot!" she finishes, handing me the binoculars.

I repeat my observation: "He's armed".

It's a light machine gun held firmly between his gloved hands, which look like an extension of his arm. He's also got some kind of large saber positioned behind his back. This guy apparently knows how to do everything. He's the ultimate cleaner. Here he is, analyzing the immediate surroundings, visually scanning the space methodically. His concentration is at a peak, ready to react to the slightest anomaly that might come his way.

His gaze lingers on every nook and cranny of the surrounding buildings, scrutinizing every window, every door with extreme meticulousness. His eyes quickly scan the surroundings, watching for the slightest suspicious movement, the slightest silhouette that might betray an unwelcome presence. A little boy runs up to him, as if to ask for something to eat.

"See that? What the hell is that kid doing here?"

"Yes, I can see that. It's not looking good...", commented Lola, glancing through the binoculars.

"Damn, did you see how he threw the kid to the ground?"

"Yes".

Mutaff kicked the little boy right in the chest. Shit, I'm losing my binoculars. That's it. The child fell several meters away, lifeless. Mutaff now approaches the little body, without hurrying. He knows he doesn't need to run. He holds out his arm with the submachine gun at the end. When he reaches the small body on the ground, he fires an endless salvo at it until his magazine is empty. With his other hand, he picks up the child's body, whose head and feet hang in the air. He approaches the dark, doorless hall of the building next door and violently throws the body inside, followed by his gun.

"He's an orphan. Little orphans don't get suspicious when they're hungry. They don't have anyone... the worst thing is to find them afterwards, devoured by dogs...", comments Lola fatalistically.

She takes my hand and squeezes it, hard.

Mutaff continues his inspection. His footsteps lead him to face our building. He stops short, his eyes riveted on our position. He hesitates for a moment, assessing the potential risks. Then, nevertheless, he continues his visual sweep in the direction of the neighboring building. His determination never wavers. He carefully examines every window, every floor, maintaining a constant scouting role, silent most of the time. His impassive face reveals nothing, concealing his intentions and emotions.

Without a word, he disengages his gaze from our block of buildings. He slowly resumes his progress along the street, then retraces his steps, lowering a second weapon.

"Shit. Did you see it? Do you think he spotted us?"

"We'll soon find out... In any case, they know we're here, somewhere," says Lola in a not very reassuring tone as she chews on an energy bar she's taken out of its bag with a crumpled paper sound. "There he is!" says Lola, pointing to the front of the armored car so I don't miss Victor's exit.

A gigantic figure emerges from the tank. The huge mass I'd identified in thermal vision is Victor's body. Shit, I was looking for a twisted little guy in a wheelchair and a metal colossus emerges.

Straightening up, he looks like some kind of robot with powerful, confident gestures. He's not at all the same frail, trembling Victor.

"It's his armor," comments Lola, less impressed than me.

"I'm dreaming..."

"Don't worry, the nightmare's coming," she concludes, giving me a completely relaxed and disillusioned glare.

What I love about Lola is that, for a given situation, you always feel the opposite emotions.

With her index finger outstretched like a corporal, she shows me a cloud of dust moving to the right behind the buildings. With a din that soon becomes deafening, a dozen light vehicles invade the square and a small army of men deploys to lock down the neighborhood.

"Is that the police?", I ask, incredulous.

"Oscar, you're delightfully funny. When was the last time you met a policeman? These are Victor's poodles. Look how well equipped they are," she points out to me, detailing the impressive amount of weaponry they carry with them.

"We won't make the grade...", I huffed, close to vertigo.

"Oscar, we've never been a match..." she snaps, rising to the table where we dumped our own weapons when we arrived.

PAUL TOSKIAM

A discreet entrance

The bank, Village of Lonesso, Maliscera region

Victor and Mutaff, like two elusive shadows, burst into the bank. Their footsteps echo down the hall as they advance, unperturbed. Their piercing eyes scan every corner of the building, ready to do battle. Customers, employees, security, all are taken by surprise as panic begins to spread. One look at the intruders and it's clear they haven't come just to say hello.

Suddenly, Victor raises his gloved hand and his fist clenches. He gives a signal to his mercenaries, who have positioned themselves in ambush in every corner of the bank. In an instant, an avalanche of masked men armed to the teeth burst from their hiding places. They surge like a tsunami over every soul in the bank.

Screams of terror and alarm sirens ring out as the great hall is transformed into a veritable battlefield. Bullets whistle through the air, windows shatter and the screams and groans of stricken victims mingle with the surrounding tumult.

Victor and Mutaff display surgical agility and precision, aided by their equipment, which does most of the work for them. With a fluid movement, Victor draws another machine gun and rains down bullets on all the unfortunates in his path. Victim after victim falls, their lifeless bodies strewn across the floor.

Mutaff, for his part, wields his saber with razor-sharp dexterity. With his twirling blade, he cleaves through the air, severing the limbs of his adversaries in a whirlwind of violence and delight. Mutilated bodies lie in his wake, paying tribute to the cruelty of his murderous art. Occasionally, he tips his hat over his head to keep it in place in this hypnotic ballet.

The infernal duo advance inexorably, forcing the employees to take refuge in the far corners of the bank. They are caught between the anvil of terror and the hammer of deafening gunfire. The walls are stained with the blood of innocents, marking the high price of their temerity.

Suddenly, a hail of bullets hits Victor head-on, but thanks to his armor, he doesn't flinch. Behind his mask, his gaze, filled with terrible fury, stares out at the horizon with a hint of contempt for his enemies. He returns a salvo on the bold man who dared to defy him and strikes him down without blinking an eye.

Mutaff, always on the move, kills relentlessly, his thirst for carnage seemingly boundless. He's hot. He wants more. He leaves no chance for anyone who crosses his path. He's the sword of chaos, the blade that purges the weak and insignificant.

As the minutes drag on like an eternity, the bursts of defense become rarer

and rarer. Cries of pain turn to agonized gasps. Victor and Mutaff's men, merciless, pour out only a few scattered shots as the bank gradually empties of life.

At last, silence reigns. With

a straight face, Victor turns to Mutaff and nods. They've accomplished their mission, eliminating every last person who was in the wrong place at the wrong time. They have thrown this honorable establishment into complete chaos, with no apparent effort.

With his hand raised, Mutaff gestures towards the men retreating to the street, while he accompanies Victor to the basement vault.

Victor and Mutaff rush through the many corridors, their footsteps echoing in the confined air.

The door to the room is wide open with bodies lying to one side. Victor's men have done a good job. The place is clean. The walls are lined with reinforced steel boxes, each compartment holding the most valuable treasures of the bank's customers, or what's left of them. Half the spaces have been ripped open. But that's not what really interests

Victor and Mutaff. They are drawn to a second room at the far end of the all-white room. Another room in which lies a mysterious black box the size of a bottle carton.

"Here we are," declares Victor in a deep, pasty voice produced by the voice generator in the mask he's wearing. "All these chests contain untold riches. But this black box is our new reason for living," he laughs.

Mutaff nods, his eyes glinting sinisterly. He's still hot, ready to kick some ass if need be. Pointing to the black box, he approaches it and says, as if inspired by the muses: "No one really knows what it contains. But its power is immense. We've heard rumors about it, and the news has spread like wildfire among the city's criminals."

Victor watches him with surprise and interest. Then, suspicious, he unloads his anger on his sidekick: "What are you talking about? Are you high again? What did you take this time?" Victor yells.

Mutaff remains silent.

"How many times have I told you that nobody gets high on a mission day? How many times have I told you? Mutaff! Shit!" growls Victor again as he hits the adjoining wall with all his might, creating a hole in the stone, leaving a trickle of splinters flowing to the floor.

Mutaff still says nothing. He knows that the next terrible blow could be for him. He knows only too well the power of this armor he himself oversaw its manufacture. He keeps silent and steps back.

Victor in turn approaches the black box, contemplating the intricate and delicate

engravings that adorn its surface. "Lola, that cunning and dangerous woman, holds the key that will allow us to open this box and reveal its secret. She should be here soon."

Mutaff sneers as he raises his hat with his fingertips to clear his forehead.

The two men stare at each other for a few moments, anticipation pulsing in their eyes. They're old brothers and both share a common goal: to seize the contents of that black box. They know that confrontation with Lola is inevitable. They know she's angry. They've taken the necessary steps. But for now, they have no choice but to wait for her arrival.

NO TREASURE FOR THE BRAVE

Listening

Village of Lonesso, Maliscera region

"Oscar, come on...", Lola offers me after fiddling with her scanner to try and pick up something in the bank. She hands me a headset, and I put one of the earpieces to my right ear and say, "I'm picking up their conversation... Listen to this..."

I take in this unusual conversation, which is almost funny, and listen attentively:

"Victor: So, Mutaff, what do you think this black box contains?

Mutaff: Oh, I'm sure it contains the ultimate power. Perhaps even a weapon of unimaginable power.

Victor: Hmm, that would be interesting. But personally, I'm leaning towards priceless treasure. Diamonds, gold, jewels... You get the idea.

Mutaff: Pfft, worthless trinkets. If it doesn't make you more powerful, it's not worth it.

Victor: Who do you think you are, putting down wealth like that? Money pays for everything, Mutaff, including you!

Mutaff: Money can also rot souls. The most powerful men are those who have absolute control, who inspire fear. Not those who juggle shiny metal coins.

Victor: Now you're a philosopher, Mutaff. This treasure can even give you back the sense of humor you once had.

Mutaff: Humor? I don't see the point in wasting my time with idle jokes anymore.

Victor: What a bore, Mutaff. Life's too short to be so serious all the time. A little levity wouldn't hurt. After all, aren't we the biggest criminal organization to emerge from this war?

Mutaff: Levity is for the weak, Victor. I prefer to concentrate on the objective and not get distracted. Number one is the most fragile position there is.

Victor: Ah, but you mustn't confuse levity with weakness, my friend. I'm talking about humor and lightness, which are the greatest manifestations of wit.

Mutaff: Trials are meant to be overcome, not laughed at.

Victor: You may be right, Mutaff. But a smile now and then never killed anyone.

Mutaff: Are you ready to die laughing, Victor?

Victor: Very funny, Mutaff. I see your sarcasm knows no bounds.

Mutaff: Sarcasm is my second language, after cruelty.

Victor: Oh, I don't need reminding. Or to teach it, as you're so fond of doing. We've already got enough on our teams!

Mutaff: Perfect, then I'll be the only one to understand all the subtleties.

Victor: Ah, maybe I should give you some competition then. We'll see who's the master of black humor!

Mutaff: Good luck, Victor. I think you need a lot of practice to compete with me.

Victor: I accept the challenge, Mutaff. At the next carnage, we'll see who's the funniest.

Mutaff: We'll see, Victor. But don't forget that nothing is more fun than hearing our enemies' cries of terror, the pleas of their wives and children, and the fire that erases their trail from this planet.

Victor: Oh, you've got poet's blood in you, Mutaff.

Mutaff: And you've got blood on you... all of you. Don't you forget it.

Victor: (thunderous laughter) Charming as ever, Mutaff. I'm glad to be able to share these moments of pure destruction with you.

Mutaff: Life's good times, right?

Victor: Absolutely, my friend. Now, let's focus on that black box. Whatever it contains, we'll do anything to get it, won't we?

Mutaff: That's right, Victor. You've already shown us your strength of character as the undisputed leader by eliminating Clara. Now it's Lola's turn. We must get her key, at all costs.

Victor: Including my death, Mutaff?

Mutaff: Including mine, Victor. We're all in this together. There's no failure in the end.

Victor: How I love the blind violence of your words, Mutaff."

Lola and I look at each other, both confused and worried by what we've just heard.

"Do you think they're...", I ask Lola, feigning naivety.

"Yes, those sons of bitches love each other!" she comments with her natural tact.

"They're a bit stupid too, aren't they? I don't know, an idea like that...", I confide, a half-smile on my lips.

"If mobsters were smart, they'd be in politics, my poor Oscar!" she exclaims, closing the scanner and folding it back into her briefcase.

"And they're on acid too, my word... Good. What do you suggest?", I ask.

"Let's do it. We kill everyone. Take the treasure. We get out...", Lola details with a confidence I take for irony. "What? Did I say something?" she asks, ingenuously.

"Two against fifty or so virile guys armed from head to toe, and two bosses who look like colossi who go through walls with a simple headbutt, sounds balanced to me."

"Any questions?" she asks.

"No."

She bursts out laughing and taps me on the shoulder. "Today, no one is counting the dead Oscar. Let's make the most of it!"

At that very moment, Lola mentally grounded me.

Yes, you've got it. At that very moment I fell head over heels in love with this woman!

I wanted to take her in my arms. I wanted to kiss her, hard, before some part of this world peels the skin off our butts. I wanted to tell her all this.

"Oscar? Are you with me?" she remarks immediately. She's like radar, that girl. She sees everything. She guesses everything.

"Yes. Everything's fine. Shall we? I'm ready."

"No. You're not ready at all. I don't want half a partner in this. What is it now? Are you thinking about Clara?" she asks, missing the mark. No, Lola, I'm not thinking about Clara. I'm not thinking about Clara anymore.

"Wait, that's it, I'm in," she continues, looking at me as if I had an elephant trunk on my forehead. "You're falling in love with me... Is that it? Is that it?" she finishes, opening her eyes wide.

"Let's say that...Let's say that...," I stammer.

"STOP! It's okay. It's okay. I get it now. So let me explain something to you Oscar. This isn't really the time or place, but we need to be very clear about this. You can't pretend to be saving the world when all you care about is my ass. No, no, no, no, no. It never works. Everyone's tried it. It just doesn't work. If your mind isn't free of that stuff, it'll never work."

"But at least I'll have a reason to go on living?", I confess.

"Honestly? Good. All right, then. I didn't think we needed to have this conversation. But it has to be. It doesn't work like that. Here's how it works, Oscar. I want total control over my sex life and reproduction. Is that clear? I want handsome, powerful, rich men vying for my attention, but only in the way and at the time that suits me. I want to be attractive when I want to be, even irresistible depending on my mood, but I don't want to be bothered by male advances when I don't want to be, especially from men I'm not interested in. I want the men I am interested in to guess my preferences and act tactfully accordingly, and I don't want any man to make the first move if I don't consider it appropriate for me. Do I make myself clear? Are you able to understand?" she asks me, after breaking my heart into a thousand pieces and torturing it in every direction.

"All right, Lola. Don't get upset. Is it like with your sister then? I'm only here because I'm the least drunk of the lot?", I tell her, a little disappointed to be dealing with just another narcissistic daddy's girl.

"Stop talking nonsense. I like you, Oscar. That doesn't mean you have to fall in love with me. I'm not a gift. I just explained that to you in detail," she said, smiling at my disappointed look.

"It's okay, I get it. You don't have to worry. There's no more ambiguity between us. I won't even try to guess. So, what exactly are we going to do about your stupid treasure? I really want to move on. Will you take out my tooth and be done with it?"

"Shit Oscar, shit! You're such a child! Now I don't trust you anymore. Imagine, we're downstairs, in a desperate situation, I'm hurt... The way you talk to me, I know you won't come to save me. You'll say to yourself, 'good riddance'. Am I wrong?"

"Listen, Lola. Since you want to, let's clear things up once and for all, okay?". She looks at me, surprised at my sharp turn. "The bidding just went up. I want 50% of the value of what we're going to find. And if I have to save you on top of that, I want 60%. That's fair, right?"

She steps back, observes me from head to toe, and steps back again, as if I've just transformed before her eyes into a gelatinous monster from interstellar space.

"Money, money, money... You're all the same, damn it!"

She sketches a mimic of disgust and a curt gesture with her hand toward the ground, as if she were throwing something in the trash. "You're forgetting one tiny detail, Oscar. Without me, you'll never know how to use the key you wear on your tooth. Do you understand that, you little fool?" she continued, trying to humiliate me to the best of her ability. "I'm the one with access to the treasure. I'm the one who decides what's good for you," she finishes, turning around and starting to put on her battle gear.

I do the same. We remain silent. Frustrated and silent. Going about our business. Each in his own corner. Like an old couple who've exhausted all their arguments. Like an old couple who hate each other, but still have a reason to exist.

PAUL TOSKIAM

Settling scores

The bank, Village of Lonesso, Maliscera region

I'm not exaggerating when I say that Lola and I are armed to the teeth. If we were to start running, some lame torture would easily overtake us.

My mouth is on fire. I've overdone it with the toothpaste. But Lola made it clear that for the key tattooed on my tooth to be operational, it had to be impeccably cleaned and accessible. Which I meticulously did. But it stings.

We're loaded with all kinds of weapons and ammunition, up to the limit of what a human being can handle. We've thought big, really big. I've got two automatic rifles strapped to my back to cut up bodies from a distance, a rocket launcher to open up walls without doors, pistols scattered all over my body to score points with between-the-eyes shooting, shurikens to slice ears like a caress of the wind, knives to slit throats, nets to block survivors, rows of ammunition to make sure we make it to the end and, above all, an indecent dose of courage, or recklessness: it's all the same.

In addition to this arrogant arsenal, Lola holds a single-button remote control firmly in her right hand. This little gadget serves as the detonator for the thermonuclear mini-bomb she wears strapped to her chest. It's an old model, but more than enough to wipe the whole village off the map. This is our ultimate argument, the one we'll use in case of misfortune when we meet Victor. And here he is: he's just come out in front of the bank to greet us.

Lola and I stand proudly a few meters in front of him, surrounded by his men. They form a circle around us with their artificial intelligence sights pointed at both our heads. The atmosphere is, how shall I say, tense?

Everyone is sizing each other up, aware of the potentially disastrous consequences of the slightest mistake.

Complete silence is the order of the day for this play that has just begun. We breathe to the accelerated rhythm of our hearts, which are well aware that we're in deep shit.

We've reached the point of no return.

Victor, like a king among his subjects, raises his hand to the heavens with grace and authority. His loyal soldiers, without a word, silently step back, their boots kicking up the brown dust on the ground. They create a sacred space around us in this critical situation. This improvised sanctuary, momentarily sheltered from danger, appears to us as a luxury revealing the high value Victor places on us in this zero-sum game.

The air is saturated with electric tension as Victor, hidden in the shadow of his imposing metal frame, uses his voice generator to greet us. His dry syllables resonate with mechanical coldness, attempting to feign cordiality. "Welcome, Lola! We've been looking forward to it," he says. It's a sign: he's ignoring me.

Positioned opposite him, she contemplates the power emanating from his armor, the personification of his now ruthless nature. "Hello, Victor. As you can see, I didn't want to miss this opportunity," she retorts, pointing to the firmly grasped remote, her thumb flirting with the liberating button.

Victor's visa is hidden behind a strange mask. His eyes twitch behind a thin groove. He analyzes the device in Lola's hand. A shiver of caution seems to run through his frame. He makes a repeated, retreating movement that, under the constraints of his exoskeleton, resembles a kind of dance.

"I see you've come with your toys?" he observes, pointing to the detonator.

His question is a poisoned kiss, disguised as a compliment. He then turns his attention to the black jumpsuit, which hugs Lola's body with a discreet sheen.

"You look delicious in that outfit, Lola," he congratulates her, slyly,

She doesn't appreciate this gravelly comment at all and raises her clenched fist around the remote again. "I didn't come here for a joke," she growls icily, her jaw clenched.

Victor moves slowly forward, reclaiming the space in front of him, making the rubble crunch under his weight. With a soothing hand, he sketches a gesture towards Lola, like a caress with which he tries to tame a wild beast. "Do you remember, Lola?" his voice crackles and hisses, caught in the electromagnetic waves of the weapons jamming the saturated air of this ramshackle square. He pauses forcibly, coughing slightly, before continuing despite the ambient electronic cacophony. "Do you remember that deserted street? Do you remember what you were about to go through? Even though your father condemned me to the chair, I was watching over you."

These words trigger the worst and force Lola back into that alley, where she knew fear. She remembers the appearance of Victor's shadow, pulling her back from the abyss. Alas, at this very moment, for Lola, this memory is like a mirage in the middle of the desert of her resentment. I stand back, without intervening. I don't want to distract her, which could weaken her further. Victor might try something.

This emotional avalanche that overwhelms her is a formidable weapon whose ravages I know well. She breathes even faster, deeper, looking for fresh air. I think I detect a slight tremor in her hand, outstretched with the detonator. For the first time, I'm afraid she's making an irrational and, above all, irreversible decision too soon.

Lola's eyes lose themselves for a moment in the shadows cast by the rusting containers, and the gutted building facades that seem to lean over us, mute witnesses to this confrontation. Lola's thumb grazes the shutter release. She raises her voice at last: "What about you, Victor? Do you remember my sister Clara, while your minions skinned her like common game?"

Victor's silhouette stands out, stiff and menacing, facing Lola like a granite statue. He's no more than a reflection of the protector he once was, now reduced to the embodiment of evil.

I can't leave Clara's hand, which is firmly gripping the metal of the detonator that can seal our fates, even by accident. I even wonder if I shouldn't calm her down. Yes, I'm scared.

I'm not the only one worried as I stare at that button with Lola's thumb drumming on it, in the midst of an emotional tornado. Victor takes a few more steps towards us, raising his arms halfway. At times, his armor makes him look like a puppet in his movements, both funny and terrifying.

"You're very clever, Lola. You've guessed the exact location of that little treasure we all covet," he bellows in his crackle-laden voice generator. Lola and I take an equal number of steps back, wary, sweeping Victor's men away with the points of our weapons.

"Obviously, you knew I was coming for this occasion, didn't you? Yes, you knew. You could have tried to double-cross me: take the loot and keep it for yourself, since you have the key," he points to me as if he's understood everything from his side too, and continues, "Yes, you could have left. You could have made this choice, without panache, but so understandable. Lola, my child..." he continues, clearly enjoying stirring the pot.

Lola concentrates. She remains silent. Me, I hold my position: I pretend I don't exist, as if I weren't there. Yet my whole being commands me to unleash the fire, to paint the walls of this village with the blood of this band of greedy morons, in short, to sign the carnage of my life.

"But you're much more subtle than that, aren't you, Lola?" resumes Victor, unfailing in his moralizing role. "You know I would have pursued you. You know I'd have found you. And you know I'd have killed you in the end for daring to betray me. Me, to whom you owe the privilege of being here, today, standing tall and valiant..." he pauses for a moment and then takes another deep, raspy breath. "I suggest we settle this matter as responsible adults, Lola," he finishes, closing his fist in front of her face.

"Your tricks don't work on me," says Lola, still brandishing her remote control.

Victor lets a few seconds pass, then lowers his fist and tries diplomacy: "If this treasure contains what we're all thinking, there'll be enough for all of us. Isn't that right, Lola?" he says at last, taking a few more steps forward.

At this distance, you can see its eyes blink and move in all directions. It calculates our positions. He calculates the possibilities. It saves time.

"One more step and we'll all take off into orbit!" shouts Lola, raising her hand from the detonator to the sky.

"Come on, come on... let's be reasonable for once. This world is tumbling into the abyss around us. Let's try not to worsen our chances of survival," explains Victor, suddenly lucid and inspired. "Our rivalries are not reason enough to destroy ourselves prematurely in a miserable mess," he concludes philosophically.

"He's bluffing," I whisper to Lola in her earpiece.

We all stare at each other once more. A gust of wind caresses our bodies and stirs Lola's blond hair, which waves above her black jumpsuit like a fiery flame. She's sublime as a warrior trying to contain her rage.

"Give me some proof," she asks Victor. "Give me proof that you're sincere and that you're not going to break this pact you're proposing," she finishes, her jaw still clenched, and raised, in defiance.

"That's the spirit! That's my girl, Lola," Victor congratulated her, drawing a monstrous automatic pistol slung at an angle from his belt.

Lola and I step back and point our guns at Victor's head, our eyes in our sights to blow him away in the next second. The mercenaries around us do the same, aiming for both our heads.

Victor shows his weapon, raising his other hand. He turns his torso back, without moving his feet. He takes aim. He fires, just once.

Mutaff's hat leaps into the air, twirls in the wind, then slowly falls back onto his face.

Mutaff's body lies in front of the bank entrance, covered by his hat.

My throat tightened and Lola almost crouched down in a defensive reflex.

Unhurriedly, Victor turns back to us, hands raised, and puts his gun away. "Will this proof do?" he asks, proud of his coup.

Time stands still for a moment, and silence falls over our tense faces, interrupted only by the wind's wail as it scatters the specks of dust in our eyes. Mutaff's body lies in definitive immobility, silent testimony to Victor's irrevocable decision. Lola, inclined, measures the weight of this gesture, seeking in this act of violence a sign of sincerity or perhaps a hidden trap. Her eyes meet Victor's. In this silent exchange, she relives the memory of conflicts, tricks and betrayals. The story between Victor and Lola is not a simple one.

I'm on my guard, aware that every heartbeat could be my last. But my trust in Lola is unshakeable. She's capable of anything, from storm to calm, from hell to negotiating with angels. Her thumb detaches itself from the detonator, but her eyes remain sharp blades, ready to strike at the slightest doubt.

For his part, Victor revels in the confusion created by his gesture. His posture reveals a tyrannical confidence, that of the great conquerors who shaped history in fury and blood. He feels he has broken into Lola's mind. He senses that she's let her guard down, opening up an unhoped-for highway. I'm familiar with the psychology of shit like Victor. Life places them in our path to remind us of ours.

"Your gesture proves your strength, Victor, but not your honor," Lola finally replies, her voice carrying in the void left by the gunshot. "Honor is not a bullet in the head of an unarmed man."

Victor's men seem to grow impatient, the barrels of their smart weapons tracking the micromovements of our bodies with menacing precision. They are ready to respond to the slightest hostility, to unleash an apocalypse of steel and fire at the slightest flaw. But they wait, because Victor's life is the fragile thread that holds them to the edge of the abyss.

"If your aim is to convince me to trust you, you're going to have to offer a lot more than a summary execution," adds Lola, her hands still ready to operate her arsenal, her voice sonorous as thunder.

Victor flashes a smile, like that of a snake revealing its game in the light. "Very well, Lola, I'll show you the true extent of my generosity," he says, addressing his men. "Stand back your weapons. Leave us alone. Lola and her companion are, for the moment, our guests." Shit: I finally exist!

The men obey, and a common retreat emanates from their military discipline. The arcs drawn by the cannons relax and curve, creating a fleeting atmosphere of relaxation within the iron circle. Lola raises her head, scrutinizing this gift of peace and gauging its price.

"Speak, Victor," she insists, "my patience has limits as deadly as your ambition," thunders Lola, completely contaminated by Victor's emphasis and overacting like a madwoman.

With a grand gesture, like a maestro in front of his orchestra at the climax of a symphony, Victor begins the last-chance dialogue. "Our rivalry, Lola, is as old as the darkness that haunts this city. But the world is changing, and we're changing with it. It's time to heal the past and forge the future. A future where you and I are allies, not enemies," Victor continues, in this battle of words.

Words that resonate, filling the void with promises and possible futures, each suspended between two flakes of dust. Lola remains impassive. Victor was right. A fragile hope rises, like a flickering sun above a devastated land, tenuous and burning. And in the silence that stretches like the string of a taut bow, Lola makes her decision.

Wounded by her past, she chooses to fight for a better future. A future that emerges from the darkness of her memories with the poignant ideals of a warrior who has chosen to believe that another world is possible.

"We're going to negotiate, Victor," she says, convinced that she has everything under control. "But let's be clear, at the slightest hint of betrayal, I won't hesitate to send us all to hell," she finishes with her remote control in hand.

The pawns are in place, the rules are clear, the final game is on.

NO TREASURE FOR THE BRAVE

The dark hall

Village of Lonesso, Maliscera region

"Orso, come and see, there's a kid!" shouts Milo as he discovers the body of a little boy who has just fallen in the building's lobby.

Orso rushes to Milo's call, his mind fogged by the hunger that keeps tugging at him. The urgency in his companion's voice still echoes in the building's dingy lobby as he discovers the macabre scene.

"Shit! A kid!" cries Orso, his wide-eyed gaze tracing circles around the frail figure lying there.

"Yes. I just told you. You're tiresome in the end, Orso. Here, have you seen the machine gun? Fuck... it weighs a ton..." grumbles Milo, his arms almost giving way under the weight of the machine gun he's struggling to lift.

"Hey, watch it! It might still have some juice in it! I don't want to end up sliced!"

Milo, vexed, holds the gun in both hands, the muscles in his forearms trembling under the tension. "Say right now I don't know how to use a gun?"

"Fucking hell, aim at something else you lunatic!" shouts Orso again, no longer containing his anger as he ducks, avoiding the direction the menacing cannon is taking.

"Silence..." orders Milo, pressing a finger against his lips in a conspiratorial gesture. "We don't want to get spotted. Shut the fuck up, will you?" he whispers, as he cautiously moves his head towards the opening overlooking the street. "Looks like the cavalry's out today!"

"Yes, it's the cops. They've come to find you. Take a good look. They're here for you!" mocks Orso as he methodically rifles through the dead child's pockets.

NO TREASURE FOR THE BRAVE

PAUL TOSKIAM

The revelation

The bank, Village of Lonesso, Maliscera region

As promised, Victor ordered all his men to leave the village. We waited for long minutes, following them on radar, until they reached a safe distance outside. Victor knows what he wants. He's also laid down all the weapons in his armor, and as a token, he's even agreed to let Lola keep her bomb and detonator, stored in a bag. Lola is a little more relaxed than she was a few minutes ago. Proof that even the most desperate situations can evolve. It's only human hubris that ruins everything. Time is a soothing pill.

But our situation is still explosive, and can probably still be derailed by Victor and Lola's every step ahead of me. We all know this. This pact is the lie we accept to survive until the treasure is opened. But once we're there, what will become of these good intentions?

At times, their shadows lengthen on the damp floor, as we move along under the bright side lights. These endless, gloomy corridors lead us into the depths of this dilapidated bank's basement. These are new sections, dug out since the start of hostilities to protect goods and people. I follow them closely. A chill runs through my hair at the sight of the shredded corpses that litter our path - macabre sentinels testifying to the clean-up operation led by Victor and Mutaff.

"You'll find...", Victor murmurs without turning around, "...that we've secured the area for your arrival", he comments like a tour guide, his fingers brushing the air in a casual gesture towards the tapestry of the dead that decorates our path.

The echo of our footsteps grows muffled as we move deeper into the bowels of the building, traversing corridors laden with secrets and shadows. The flickering lights now struggle to combat the darkness clinging to the bare, oozing stones of the walls. We soon arrive before a massive door, whose intricate locking devices hint at the importance of what lies behind.

With a theatrical bow, Victor pushes open the door, which swings open with a solemn creak. He bends slightly, to be the first to enter this antechamber of mystery.

The vault, larger than it looks from the outside, is bathed in immaculate white. We follow Victor's lead, indicating a second door at the far end. He pushes it open, as easily as the first, and bows his head again to pass through. We enter this new room, almost identical to the previous one, but with no chests on the walls. Our eyes instinctively scan every nook and cranny of this white room, adorned with refined, intricate ornamentation that runs along the walls and meets at the ceiling, recalling the splendor of a bourgeois apartment of yesteryear. A small period washbasin, accompanied by a finely chiselled silver-framed mirror, sits elegantly against a wall, catching the delicate light.

At the center of the room stands a gleaming white antique chest of drawers, whose curved legs and meticulous craftsmanship testify to the skill of the master cabinetmakers who devoted their art to it. On top of this exceptional piece of furniture rests a strikingly contrasting black box. Its enigmatic appearance is accentuated by the mortuary glow of the indirect, subdued lights that diffuse through the space, giving it an almost mystical appearance.

"Lola, Oscar, dearest ones, contemplate the elusive splendor!" enthuses Victor as he begins to turn around the black box enthroned in the center of the room. It is the enigma that reigns supreme over the silence of the place.

The box, a perfect cube, seems to drink in all the light around it, an abysmal object that dwarfs the brilliance of the subdued lighting and greedily devours the slightest ray that dares to venture onto its reflection-free surface. As I approach, to enjoy the spectacle too, a feeling of inexorable tension takes hold of my senses. It's as if my whole being knew in advance that none of us would make it out of this place alive. I shake my head to regain my composure and dispel this vision of anguish. I swallow my saliva hard and start coughing in increasingly sonorous jerks, as if I were about to spit toads.

"Are you all right?" worries Lola, discovering my defeated face and eyes reddened by the effort of expulsion.

I nod my head with a triumphant smile, like a conqueror who has just conquered a hilltop. My lips stretch in satisfaction, reflecting the glow of a colossal intimate victory. Victor in turn turns to me, with an air of "What did your buddy here take before he came?". He's very strict about hygiene.

I manage to catch my breath and wipe my forehead. With a wave of my hand I let them know that, in all probability, I should survive. Victor approaches and puts his hand on my shoulder: "Hang in there, buddy, we're gonna need you!"

Lola told her about my tattooed tooth. My shoulder's out. His armor is massive.

"So, what's in this wonderful box?" murmurs Victor, his intonation imbued with solemnity, adopting the posture of an initiate about to discover a secret of the gods. Behind his mask, his sparkling eyes betray his insatiable curiosity, which culminates in an interminable hunt, while his deliberately hushed, synthetic voice gives the meeting the air of an occult ceremony.

"No one still alive has the answer," confirms Lola with a wave of her hand, inviting me to equip myself with the most eccentric accessory mankind has devised: the mouth spreader.

I carefully remove it from my pocket and set it up. She bends down to help me adjust this special model, making sure that my tattooed tooth stands out. Victor watches me for a moment, with interest, before bursting into laughter. It's a prolonged laugh that makes him bend over and slap his thighs in unbridled hilarity. His muffled laughter spreads throughout the room. Straightening up, he tries to pat me on the shoulder as a sign of camaraderie, but I duck deftly, avoiding his friendly gesture by the skin of my teeth. His voluminous hand splits the air before me, generating a gust of wind that sweeps across my face. My shoulder escaped the worst.

At that very moment, our hearts miss a beat. A tremendous tremor shakes the room, vibrating the very foundations of the building above us. We remain petrified, paralyzed by the sudden magnitude of the detonation. Our eyes meet in a whirlwind of surprise, fear and suspicion. A shiver runs through us. Has our pact been betrayed?

Victor is about to speak when a second brutal vibration shakes the building with devastating intensity, surpassing the previous tremor. The lights flicker feverishly, projecting discontinuous flashes that dance on the walls, like an ominous warning of their imminent failure. Darkness threatens to engulf us at any moment. In the chaos, the door has been violently slammed shut, and an acoustic pressure assails our eardrums, as sharp as a blade.

Victor observes and scans every nook and cranny of the ceiling, as if looking for a clue. "They're shelling the area. We've got to hurry," Victor articulates, urgency tinging his voice as he approaches the chest of drawers as if to take away the mysterious box.

Lola, her forehead wrinkled with distrust, moves close enough to Victor for his foul breath to pass through the filter of her mask. She takes a step back from the unbearable smell, then asks: "What are you playing at, Victor?" she says, her jaw clenched and raised at him.

Victor's voice generator begins to crackle again as he stares at the box. "I'm playing to get out of here alive, just like you. Word of a valuable treasure in this village must have spread like wildfire," he says thoughtfully, pausing for a moment before resuming: "Secrets are made to be revealed, aren't they?" he laughs, still pointing at the black box. "No more time to lose if we don't want to end up under the rubble, flattened like pancakes," he finishes, while my saliva drips down my cheek all the way to my neck thanks to that infernal mouth spreader.

Lola looks at me, puzzled, as I try to find the right posture. She approaches me to guide me into the perfect position, leaning slightly over the black box, my face turned to my right shoulder. "Try not to move," she asks me as she pulls out a small flashlight to shine on my tooth.

"And so this tooth will open the box?" asks Victor, incredulous.

No sooner do Victor's last words vanish into thin air than the box begins to shake, emitting a constant low-frequency hum, like an engine awakening from a mechanical torpor. A bit like me in the morning.

Victor, startled by the sudden animation, instinctively steps back, his eyes wide with incomprehension. "What's that thing?" he asks.

Lola, whose piercing gaze betrays no fear, gives me the imperative sign to remain motionless. Every beat of my heart resounds in my chest with force, as if trying to throw me off balance. I try to hold my breath, while fighting the anguish rising up inside me, this frightening feeling that this unpredictable object is going to explode in a thousand splinters in my face. I always assume the worst, it's the story of my life.

Victor, as if dazed and weighed down by the burden of his armor, staggers, unbalanced by his unexpected retreat. He beats the air with his arms, desperately searching for a hold to regain his balance. "We're almost there," Lola murmurs in a voice brimming with a quiver of excitement, her lamp aimed with surgical precision at my exposed tooth. The trembling light seems to give life to the box, which vibrates with an increasingly intense energy, giving the menacing illusion of being equipped with multiple invisible eyes, alive and scrutinizing.

Victor, his eyes wide with astonishment, stares at the box as it metamorphoses before us, taking on a spherical shape as perfect as it is unusual. "Shit, is it alive?" he murmurs, a hint of fascination mingling with his amazement. He can't suppress an excited cry, his curiosity colliding with his disbelief. "What the fuck is it?" he blurts out in panic.

In the urgency of the moment, Lola gives him a look that's as scathing as the silence she demands. "Shut up, dammit!" she hisses, all her attention riveted on my tooth. A searing pain shoots through me, concentrated around my tooth, so intense that I could swear an invisible force is trying to extract it from my jaw. And in this whirlwind of frantic sensations, it becomes clear to me that this cursed box, with its changing shape, is yearning for something even more personal: this bitch wants my tooth back.

The pain turns into unbearable torment in the fleeting instant of a wink. My head, as if caught in the clutches of an evil will, is irresistibly drawn towards the vibrating sphere. It's an occult, indomitable force, against which my struggles are in vain.

Lola, understanding the urgency of the moment, gives Victor an imperative sign, urging him to join her in holding my body. I close my eyes in terror. Eyelids closed, I feel the icy touch of Victor's armor. He hugs my chest firmly with his massive arm and places his other strong hand on my forehead, following Lola's precise instructions: "Hold it like that! It's almost over," she murmurs, turning off her flashlight.

Suddenly, my whole head begins to vibrate, echoing the sphere's movements. Victor's strong hand struggles to contain my forehead, but the struggle proves futile.

Subtly, I slide forward and my mouth collides head-on with the black sphere, sealing a macabre kiss with this vibrating object. Victor struggles to pull me back, seeking to break the forced union between the sphere and me, ready to decapitate me if need be. But Lola, with the authority of someone who has already witnessed such supernatural events, intervenes: "No, stop! It's too risky", she asserts, immersed in intense contemplation, her thoughts racing towards memories or knowledge of her own. In an almost solemn voice, she proclaims, "She's going to take his tooth..."

My mind has given up, overwhelmed by the excruciating pain that now consumes me from head to toe. My body begins to tremble in concert with the sphere, in a duet carried by an unknown energy. My mouth is pressed against the fiery ball with increasing intensity, hinting at the frightening sensation that it could swallow me whole. I let out a heart-rending scream, a mixture of agony and horror, while Lola and Victor stand there, helpless or resigned, like frozen silhouettes, accomplices in an unspeakable torture. In this most tragic of postures, as the lights fade and flicker like dying stars and the building rumbles and shakes again under the onslaught of the apocalypse outside, my panicked gaze catches the outline of an enigmatic smile on Lola's lips.

She had me fooled. She never told me I was going to have a barbaric dental session without anesthesia. I feel like she's reading my mind.

"Oscar... I didn't know...", she tries to console me when suddenly the force holding my mouth pressed against that sphere disappears and I fall back to the ground like a lump, exhausted.

Immediately, Victor rushes to help me up, his firm hands gripping my shoulders to turn me to face his monstrous mask. I spit my spreader, which bounced off him. He doesn't appreciate it. The pain that overwhelms me is now accompanied by a horrific vision, that of his masked face whose outline fails pitifully to reproduce the slightest trace of humanity. "You're bleeding," he observes with almost amused detachment. I can feel his eyes analyzing me with the intensity of a pair of overheated surveillance cameras. "I know, you big piece of junk," I say with the sarcasm of my exhaustion, the taste of blood in my mouth.

In my confusion, the room has changed without my noticing. The walls are now swept with dancing sparkles, like those of a disco ball in the heart of a dizzy disco. Gradually coming to my senses, I sit up straighter and look into Lola's face. I discover her absolutely fascinated by the source of these hypnotic reflections. But it's not a disco ball, no. If we'd come all this way for that, I think we'd want to smash everything.

A translucent gemstone of gigantic proportions sits before us in a moment of unearthly silence, beautifully poised on the dresser where that black sphere should have been.

What is the mystery behind this stone, balanced like a translucent obelisk defying the laws of nature?

"No! Don't touch!" screams Lola as Victor brings his index finger close to the giant gemstone.

"It's a..." stammers Victor, salivating as if at the sight of a confection.

"A diamond...", completes Lola.

"It's big!" comments Victor, rubbing his hands together.

"Who's holding it up like that?", I ask intrigued by this spine-chilling magic, sponging my mouth with the compresses Lola hands me.

"Nobody," she decides, as bewildered as Victor and me.

"The hen laid a big egg!" comments Victor as he grabs the giant diamond with both hands, unthinkingly, buoyed by his plundering instincts.

"SHIT! VICTOR!" screams Lola, nearly choking.

"What? Look, I'm holding him in my arms, this big baby!" exclaims Victor, carefully caressing the gigantic sphere-cut diamond. "He loves it, the bugger! And then, what a weight, this rascal!". Victor then straightens up, back arched, as if celebrating a major success.

"Who could have carved that?", I ask while wiping my brow and painfully swallowing a powerful painkiller. "I mean, someone must have unearthed it in the rough and carved it to a high standard - it's wonderful..."

"You're right. We expected the exceptional. And we're not disappointed, are we?" intervenes Lola, moving closer to the stone to touch it in turn. I can see her smile crossing her face like sunshine.

"We'll have to make suitable tools to cut this giant and then deal with the sharing!", Victor is already thinking aloud, calculating the profit he could smuggle in, once the treasure has been reduced to small stones.

"LET'S HOPE THERE'S SOMETHING LEFT!" calls a voice from the doorway that has just opened.

A raggedly dressed vagrant enters, staggering under the weight of the heavy machine gun he brandishes with difficulty in our direction, quickly joined by a companion. "Perhaps I can help you carve the baby?" he sneers, pointing the barrel at the diamond.

Carefully, Victor rests the diamond on the chest of drawers with Lola's help. The stone stops floating and settles in balance on one of its small facets. "Who are you? What do you want?" calls Victor, trying to mask his vulnerability with an authoritative synthetic voice, and cursing himself for having agreed to keep his men away, who would have made short work of these two clowns.

"Damn, you sound like a duck, man!" comments Lilo, hilarious at the sound of Victor's synthetic voice. "I'm Lilo. And this is Orso," introduces the machine-gun-wielding vagabond. "We were having a quiet rest, when your explosions and your merry-go-round disturbed us a bit," he laughs, waving the barrel of the submachine gun in front of him.

"Put the gun down or you'll regret it!" threatens Victor.

"Hey, calm down duck!" retorted Lilo, leaning back to raise the barrel of his gun toward Victor. "What was I saying? Ah yes, so Orso and I thought you hadn't come with all these people just to say hello to the bank employees, eh? Didn't we, Orso?" he laughs, while Orso nods complicitly, finishing gulping down a piece of grilled meat.

"Where does this meat come from?" questions Victor, astonished to discover that common vagrants possess such a rare commodity.

"Oh, this? That's the guy who was showing off with his cowboy hat. He gently swung it at us. We

didn't even have to shoot him to enjoy it!" replies Orso with a greasy laugh, raising his piece of meat in salute.

No sooner had Orso finished his sentence than Lola, in a fit of rage, understanding the unspeakable, rushed at him, ready to hit him with all her might. But Victor, in a burst of lucidity, holds her back, pointing at the threatening machine gun and Lola's bag containing the mini-bomb.

Alas, frightened out of her wits, Lilo pulls the trigger and an avalanche of bullets lacerates Lola's flesh and bone diagonally, sending her tumbling backwards with a thud. The top of the diamond wobbles under the impact before it too falls piteously to the ground. Victor's left arm, caught in this storm of metal, shatters, releasing a shrill synthetic cry of pain.

"Shit, I hit the duck!" laughs Lilo, his cutting mockery merging with Orso's cynical sneer. "Folks, I'm truly sorry. This weapon is a monster, too heavy for me. It goes off like that, without warning, and I don't know how to aim," he confesses, still sweeping the gun barrel in front of him, poorly concealing the shiver of caustic laughter that shakes him in a sinister echo of the horror he's just spilled across the white room, now flecked with red, blood red.

"Here, you cocksucker...", Lilo looks at my swelling distorted mouth. "You're going to help us get the rock out of here," he orders me, pointing to the diamond on the floor with the end of his cannon.

"You can't escape, you little shit. My men will tear you to pieces up there!" threatens Victor as he straightens up after his fall, attempting a last-ditch bluff. Lola lies inert, gutted on the ground.

"Your buddies? What mates are you talking about? It's quiet up there as you say. The special forces have made good housekeeping." He turns to Orso, with a knowing and amused wink, reloading his weapon. "Did you think I was going to fall for your little crap? Ugly duckling!" taunts Lilo, resuming his endless laughter, always followed by Orso's as he approaches the diamond to handle it.

Victor was furious. He straightens up and lunges at Lilo, who is emptying his magazine at full height. In the din and smoke of the bullets cutting into him, he turns to me. I see his eyes, agitated, distraught, saddened, catch mine in a helpless farewell. What is this weapon capable of piercing his carapace? Victor falls backwards. The impact unlocks part of his armor's fastenings and blows off his mask.

"Damn, he's as ugly as a hen's ass!" observes Orso as he approaches Victor's body to begin searching it.

Strangely enough, I don't feel any fear. It must be this sedative that has switched off all the receptors in my body, including my brain.

"Come on, let's get moving!", Lilo orders me again while I watch him, almost fascinated by his luck. He notices and sneers : "Sorry, no treasure for the brave this time! You take the rock and we'll get out of here. Then I'll shoot you when you load this into the truck," he explains, waving the barrel in front of me, threatening to put me through the chopper.

PAUL TOSKIAM

A picturesque little village

Village of Lonesso, Maliscera region

No doubt motivated by Lilo's exploits, Orso approaches me and slaps me across the face, urging me to follow his accomplice's orders to the letter.

And yet, frankly, I'm sick of this whole circus. I'm sick of this war. I want my fucking breakfast!

Why did I let myself get caught up in the madness of these people? Ah, yes, that unusual diamond. I don't know. That's where the hope of easy money took me. I hate myself.

I pretended to obey and crouched down to pick up the diamond. But all the better to bounce off Orso. I pick him up and hold him in front of me with outstretched arms. His feet no longer touch the ground.

Just as I thought, Lilo pulls the trigger again and fires in my direction. Between my arms, I can see Orso's ugly face: bullets aren't his thing. I immediately throw him at Lilo with all my might before the bullets start hitting me.

Lilo is thrown off balance by Orso's body, which falls on top of him and shoots in all directions, perforating a good part of the room's walls and ceiling. I take advantage of this to roll on the floor and knock him off balance, then break his legs. It's my signature move. Lilo cries out as if I'm cutting her throat. Ah? yes, sorry, I've just slit his throat with the little dagger I borrowed from the side pocket of his pants.

There's still some grumbling in the white room, whose ceiling threatens to collapse at any moment, with streams of white dust pouring out and debris starting to come loose. I take one last look at this place of woe.

I approach Lola, atrociously mutilated, like her sister. I take a long look at her. It's ugly how shredded she is. I don't even recognize her angelic face anymore, turned into an absolutely terrifying rictus. I think I loved her. I mean, I don't know. I'll decide later.

I grab his bag, empty it of all his belongings and plunge the diamond into it, which struggles to get in: he like me, it's not so big, it's heavy. It must be tens of thousands of carats, in other words, this thing is worth millions. I don't know why, but I'm sure the guy who cut this diamond doesn't live in this part of the galaxy. Just a thought. Have you ever seen a tooth-eating diamond?

I also retrieve the detonator and slip it into my trouser pocket. You never know, it might come in handy.

I slung the loaded bag over my shoulder and grabbed the heavy, blood-spattered submachine gun. I also retrieve the two remaining magazines from the inside pockets of Lilo's jacket. He was the brains behind this little army of two opportunists. He needs a little more practice on the range, I think. In the next life, anyway.

I leave this cursed room, firing into the air until I've emptied the clip to help the ceiling collapse.

I run through the corridors like a maniac. Soon I hear the roar of stone doing its work, lower down behind me.

Lilo and Orso had planned it well, the buggers. The truck is parked in front of the bank entrance. They were right: there's carnage all around. All I can make out are the remains of human bodies. More like pools of blood, thickened by the remains of shreds of flesh. I can see Victor's armored car, completely upturned and gutted. There's no doubt that whoever did this was after him, looking for something. Strange that they came away empty-handed... It must have been a bunch of youngsters on a secret escapade who were curtly called to order by their hierarchy. I've been there.

Well, does this truck have a working engine? I inspect it, going all the way round as a precaution. You can never be too careful. Nobody on board, nobody around, nobody in the vicinity, the driver's cab door almost opens by itself. All right: clear zone.

I can't help smiling as I climb into the back. Orso and Lilo had retrieved an old trunk and straps to attach it to the hooks on the sides of the truck. At least they had a sense of logistical organization: real scavengers. Frankly, thanks guys! What's more, without knowing it, you've hit the nail on the head: the bag with the diamond fits perfectly in your trunk! I'm still laughing, my mouth swollen. I wipe away a tear and waste no more time. I tighten the straps to secure the precious cargo and close the truck's rear doors, carefully tucking the trunk key into my trouser pocket.

Come to think of it, I kind of liked it. Lonesso is a picturesque little village that I'd recommend to anyone looking for a few days' rest. It's the ideal place to have breakfast, in the peace and quiet of the countryside.

I walk the few steps to the cockpit, holding the submachine gun in one hand and massaging my still-sore mouth with the other. All I want to do right now is go back to bed!

I open the door to climb into the cab and take the wheel. But my gaze locks on the three prongs of the arrow cocked in the harpoon-gun held tightly by the old crone from the hotel. His face is even more screwed up than mine. I recognize the same three prongs and the same harpoon gun as Victor's. I look her straight in the eye. I look straight at her. I make a move to dodge and point my submachine gun at her head. She smiles at me with a hint of regret on her puffy face.

"Thanks for the cargo," she says, releasing the arrow that comes to plant itself squarely in my chest, propelling me out of the cabin.

I fall backwards, unable to move and drop my weapon in the fall. This thing really hurts my plexus. I hear footsteps nearby and someone leans over me. It's the driver. Fuck, it's the driver! What's he doing here? With a face even more bruised than the old lady's?

He inspects me with his eyes, as if to make sure the arrow is in the right place. He frowns. Then, with a precise gesture, he presses down on the arrow with all his weight. I feel the metal pierce the rest of my ribcage until it crunches into the earth behind my back. What the hell is this son of a bitch playing at? I writhe in excruciating pain as he rifles through my trouser pockets for the small key to the safe. I'd have taken his head off a second time.

The taste of blood returns, abundant, to my mouth and I hear the truck speed off, leaving behind a cloud of brown dust.

I gaze up at the pristine blue sky, while dust covers my eyes as it falls on me. The universe has crashed. But the old lady won't take the treasure with her.

I take advantage of my last breath to bring my hand close to the detonator and press the button.

THE END

Did you love *No Treasure for the Brave*? Then you should read *She Bites Zombies*[1] by Paul Toskiam!

[2]

Delve into the horror of a devastated world The truth? Zombies don't exist... until you become one.Lana thought she was living an ordinary life, but everything changed in a split second. In a world where nightmares come to life, she discovers the horror of her transformation: one bite, and everything changes.**A cursed power**Now a zombie, Lana realizes that her bites have a terrifying power: they can heal other victims of this apocalypse. But this gift makes her a target for those who seek to exploit her incredible potential.**Countess Miranda: An insidious threat**In the shadows, Countess Miranda, an enigmatic aristocrat and former escort, prepares sinister plans. Her flamboyant palace hides unspeakable secrets, and she will do anything to seize

---

1. https://books2read.com/u/47BARR

2. https://books2read.com/u/47BARR

Lana's power. What is hidden behind her charming smile?**A romance in the heart of despair**In the midst of chaos, Lana meets Jon, a mysterious man whose attraction is as captivating as it is distressing. Together, they navigate a world where trust is rare and every decision can be fatal.**Do you dare to discover what lurks in the darkness?**- Guaranteed chills: Every page will immerse you in an oppressive atmosphere.- Unbearable suspense: The shocking revelations will leave you speechless.- A fight for survival: Between love and danger, every moment counts.**Prepare to be captivated**Order "She Bites Zombies" today and lock yourself in a safe place. Once immersed in this story, you will no longer be able to escape the horrors that lurk behind every dark corner.- What you'll experience: Why you can't miss this novel- Palpable tension: You'll be kept in suspense until the last page- Tormented characters: Their struggle will resonate with you- A chilling ending: Prepare to be shockedDon't let the shadows catch up with you. Jump in and face your fears!

Also by Paul Toskiam

About the Author

Discover the captivating universe of PAUL TOSKIAM, the master of the extraordinary infiltrating the ordinary. With a voracious pleasure for turning mundane situations into thrilling adventures, he will make you reevaluate your certainties and completely shake up your perspective.

Forget about traditional patterns because with PAUL TOSKIAM, you will be drawn into extraordinary plots where tension is palpable on every page turned. The heroes and villains are not who you think they are. It's what will drive you crazy, but also what you'll love.

But that's not all, subtle and irresistible humor is one of PAUL TOSKIAM's trademarks. His characters come to life with realism, becoming endearing and unpredictable, adding a unique touch to each story.